RESISTING NICOLE

THE KINCAID SERIES

BOOK 3

BJ Wane

Copyright © 2024 by BJ Wane
All rights reserved.

This book or any portion thereof may not be reproduced or used in any manner whatsoever without the express written permission of the author except for the use of brief quotations in a book review.

Editors:
Kate Richards & Nanette Sipes

Cover Design & Formatting:
Joe Dugdale (sylv.net)

Disclaimer

This contemporary romantic suspense contains adult themes such as power exchange and sexual scenes. Please do not read if these offend you.

Dedication

This book is dedicated to Joe Dugdale and Sylv Kerslake at sylv.net who work on my book covers & formatting as well as my social media marketing, and to my editors Kate Richardson and Nanette Sipes

I couldn't do it without you!

CONTENTS

Chapter One 7
Chapter Two 31
Chapter Three 55
Chapter Four 79
Chapter Five 101
Chapter Six 125
Chapter Seven 147
Chapter Eight 171
Chapter Nine 195
Chapter Ten 219
Chapter Eleven 239
Chapter Twelve 261
Chapter Thirteen 283
Epilogue 305

About BJ Wane 311
More Books by BJ Wane 313
Contact BJ Wane 315

Chapter One

"Please, Tony, I'm begging you. P-put the knife down."

Nicole's voice shook as much as her hand. To steady her grip on the gun, she brought up her sliced arm, keeping her eyes on Tony instead of watching her blood drip onto the white bedroom carpet. Her neck, collarbone, and the right side of her breast burned from the downward slash he'd managed when she'd come out of the attached bathroom not expecting this volatile about-face from before she'd taken a shower. *My fault, not his.* She kept repeating that to stay focused. Otherwise, she would give in to the pain and despair of his condition.

A week ago, the doctors had warned her, Tony, and his siblings his brain tumor was growing again, and how that would impact his mood swings and cognizance of his surroundings. When Tony bought her the gun six months ago, right after his diagnosis, neither of them could have known how soon she would need to use it to defend herself against him.

"What do you want? Money, jewelry?" he sneered, advancing with a maniacal glint in his dark eyes. Waving the large blade stained with her blood, he acted as if the gun she held was of no consequence. "How did you get in my house? I-I have..." Tony frowned, his face showing confusion before the pain-induced rage returned and he lunged for her.

Nicole cried out and jumped back to avoid another agonizing injury. Now she was cornered between the bed where they had shared so many hours of pleasure and the window with a view of his beautiful landscaped yard. Shaking inside and out, she prayed he would become lucid again soon.

"Tony, it's me, Nicole. I live here with you, remember? We went to the lake yesterday and picked up your favorite pizza on the way home."

When these paranoid memory lapses

first started, his doctors told her to remind Tony of recent events. That had worked until today. For the last thirty minutes, she'd tried everything she could think of, starting with their afternoon spent sailing, Tony's favorite pastime, and going back three years to when they first met. She hoped repeating yesterday's excursion would trigger his recognition long enough for Nicole to grab her phone out of her purse lying on the chair.

"You're lying. I don't know you." He brandished the knife then gazed at the red-stained blade with a confused frown, paying no attention to the gun or her for several moments.

Taking advantage of his distraction, Nicole tried to slip by him, inching along the wall until she came to the window. The sun had still been shining when she'd come upstairs, but now, nightfall darkened the room, casting everything into shadow.

"You do know me, Tony. I'm Nicole." Her arms turned heavy, aching, the cuts burning like acid and making her nauseous, but she didn't dare let her guard down. That's how he'd gotten her neck and shoulder.

Praying for strength, she took in the weight he'd lost since he was diagnosed with an inoperable brain tumor. His six-foot-four, two-hundred-fifty-pound frame had shrunk rapidly, the tumor growing at an alarming rate, much quicker than they were first told. The faster he declined, the more his siblings fought with her over his care. She was physically and emotionally drained but wouldn't walk away when he needed her most.

His face cleared, and he looked at her with lucidity. "Nicole? My head hurts."

"I know," she said, breathing easier when he started to lower the knife. "Let me get to the phone and call for help, Tony. They can give you something for the pain." She realized her mistake right away, forgetting he didn't trust anyone during these episodes.

"No!"

Tony lunged, coming at her with the knife raised. With nowhere to go, fear and self-preservation took over, and she pulled the trigger the same moment searing pain engulfed her left side. He gazed at her in stunned surprise that changed to profound relief before collapsing against her and then to the floor, his blood-soaked chest not moving. Ignoring her own injuries, she went to her knees, sobbing, not willing to accept she'd killed the man who meant so much to her.

"Oh God, no, please. Tony, don't die, please don't die," she begged, searching for a pulse but already knowing she wouldn't find one. Ignoring the agony of her injuries, she scrambled up and crawled across the bed then fumbled in her purse for the phone.

The rest of the evening and night passed in a blur of shock and pain for Nicole. Even doped up on meds, she couldn't forget the look on Tony's face, that split second of peaceful calm and love before he died in her arms. She'd held his hand when the test results had come back and they listened to the specialist lay out his prognosis, and then argued with him when he called his attorney and gave her medical power of attorney. She'd never wanted the responsibility of choosing life or death for anyone, let alone someone she cared about.

Now, it didn't matter, since she killed

him.

Nicole rolled over in the uncomfortable hospital bed and gazed at the unappealing skyline of downtown Chicago. She supposed, if someone liked city views, Chicago had some of the best, or so she'd heard growing up. Hailing from the wrong side of the tracks in the poorer part of the city, she never shopped or ate anywhere near the high-rises outside her window until she met Tony Renaldi of *the* Renaldis. Tears pricked her eyes as she recalled bumping into him as she walked out of the animal shelter with a dog in need of exercise.

✷✷✷✷✷

"Ooops, sorry."

Nicole looked up at the man she hadn't seen just outside the animal shelter's door. He was dressed in an expensive three-piece suit, and she took him for a bigwig at one of the corporate headquarters a few blocks away, the exact type of man she had no use for. Now that she'd apologized, her first inclination was to rush by him as he held the door open, ignoring anything he had to say. There was no time in her day to waste on polite chitchat with anyone, or to indulge in flirtatious come-ons, which she suspected he was about to start when he smiled.

Gritting her teeth, she'd stepped past him when he surprised the heck out of her and asked, "Hey, is this fella up for adoption? He's just what I'm looking for."

"You were going inside?" She thought he'd seen her at the glass door. Sam, the mixed-breed stray with a wiry black coat and floppy ears, pressed closer to Nicole's leg. "Yes, he is, but he's very timid and needs a quiet home."

The man squatted down and held his hand out to Sam. "I live alone, so it doesn't get much quieter. Good boy." He praised Sam for sniffing his fingers then straightened and pointed to her name tag. "Do you volunteer a lot here?"

"When I can, and I need to walk him. If you're interested in Sam, tell Linda at the desk."

Nicole pivoted and started toward the

corner crosswalk, her curiosity piqued, but not enough to linger. He surprised her again as he joined her instead of entering the shelter. Most men walked away when she didn't follow their cue and engage in conversation or show interest in them.

"Do you mind if I tag along to get to know him better first?"

She cast a quick glance his way and noticed his attention was on Sam and not her. Now her curiosity needed appeasing. "No, but judging by your appearance, you could likely afford a pedigreed dog or one of the fancy doodle designer pets. Why do you want a mutt?"

They stopped at the crosswalk, and he pushed the button before focusing on her with his head cocked. "Didn't anyone ever tell you not to judge a book by its cover?"

Smiling at him for the first time, she replied, "Just the opposite. My mother was always telling me what you see is usually what you get. That went doubly for people."

The Walk sign lit up, and he didn't say anything else until they reached the park on the other side. "So, you pegged me for a spoiled rich guy and are cynical enough to question why I'm slumming at the local shelter?"

Nicole shrugged. Let him believe she was shallow and judgmental. What did she care? He took the leash from her, switched it to his other hand, and clasped hers, saying, "It looks like I'll have to convince you both I'm a nice guy worth getting to know."

*****

Nicole held out her bandaged arm, remembering the man who had been worth getting to know, not who he had become due to circumstances beyond his control. Tony spent an hour with her and Sam that afternoon then filled out the adoption papers before leaving. After learning he was the youngest of the elite, wealthy Renaldis, she'd tested his sincerity in wanting to get to know her when he asked her out. She would never forget her astonishment when he agreed to meet her at Bob's Pizza, a small, family-owned pizzeria located in her old neighborhood. He'd arrived wearing jeans and a Mets T-shirt, looking genuinely happy to see her, leaving her no choice but to admit she was wrong to stereotype him. Tony Renaldi had been the nicest, most down-to-earth guy she'd ever met. She'd loved living with him, his unwavering support and encouragement these last two years while she finished college, and the way he stood up for her against his siblings constant attacks.

"No charges – no way in hell! Let me in there, damn you! I want that bitch who killed my brother to face me."

Speaking of Tony's siblings. Nicole sighed and sat up, wincing at the pull on the stitches in her shoulder and side. Natalie, Tony's twin, was always the most vocal about her disapproval of Nicole and Tony's relationship. She hated sharing her brother with anyone, especially someone she deemed so unsuitable for both Tony and the Renaldi name. She strained to hear what the nurses were telling Natalie, then a deeper, more authoritative voice seeped through the door.

"You'll have to come with me, ma'am, and I insist you keep your voice down."

Natalie's arguments faded, and Nicole assumed security was escorting her out. When the police knocked and entered with her doctor a few minutes later, she figured they had explained the circumstances of Tony's death, at least what she remembered telling them last night in the emergency room as pictures of her injuries were taken. She recognized the dark-haired, blue-eyed detective who had taken her statement, recalling the comfort of his compassion and assurances.

"Ms. Wells, do you remember me from last night? Detective Washburn."

"Yes, I do, Detective. I heard Tony's sister." She switched her attention to the doctor who'd visited her earlier that morning. "When can I leave?"

"Today, if you'd like. You can have your stitches removed in the ER or by your doctor at a follow-up in two weeks. I'll send you home with antibiotic and pain med prescriptions."

The doctor wrote in her chart as Detective Washburn came up to the side of the bed. "I hate to tell you this, but the family is going to give you grief over their brother's death. We already have a report from Tony's oncologist, who verified the tumor and his escalating violent behavior due to the growing pressure in his head. Your injuries confirm you acted in self-defense, and you're cleared of any wrongdoing. I have to ask, though, why you stayed, given the risk?"

Nicole tensed, finding the inquiry offensive, forcing herself to remain calm and unaffected before answering stiffly, "I don't walk away from people I care about when they need me the most."

They both gazed at her with a measure of respect, the detective sighing then squeezing her good shoulder. "Society would be better off with more people like you, willing to make sacrifices for others."

Uncomfortable with praise, she shifted on the bed and turned her head toward the window again. "Yes, well, as it turned out, my staying didn't help Tony. Just the opposite."

"Or maybe it was a blessing he went fast instead of dying a slow, painful death," the doctor said, closing her chart. "I'll sign your discharge papers. Take care."

Detective Washburn waited until the

doctor left before telling her, "Natalie has been escorted out, and Michael and Douglas left with her. At least they tried to get her calmed down and under control, and showed no animosity toward you when I explained Tony's attack. You have every right to refuse to see them, but I would advise you to move out of Tony's house as soon as you can."

Michael Renaldi, the eldest, had been the least vocal about objecting to her relationship with Tony, treating her with detached politeness, as if his little brother's affairs were of no consequence. Douglas flat-out ignored her, and Natalie was in her face every chance she got. From what she recalled last night, the detective had thought it best to inform the family of Tony's death early this morning instead of after midnight when he'd left the ER.

"I plan to," Nicole replied, relieved not to face Tony's siblings today. "My parents will pick me up when I'm dismissed and help me. I'll be out later today with our dog." She hardened her tone. "I won't leave Sam."

"If any of them make a stink about that, let me know." He handed her his card. "Call me if they give you trouble. Otherwise, take care of yourself, Ms. Wells."

"I will. Thank you, Detective." She would start by vowing not to get emotionally involved again. She hadn't been in love with Tony but couldn't imagine the pain of losing him, especially under these circumstances.

All Nicole wanted now was to get Sam and heal at her parents' house before making a decision on where to go from here.

*****

"Damn it, Michael, you might be the oldest, but you can't boss me around anymore. Let me go!" Natalie Renaldi yanked her arm out of her brother's hold and swiped at the tears cascading down her grief-ravaged face.

Michael glared at her, his emotions in as much turmoil as his sister's, then cast a look around the hospital parking lot, relieved no one stood gawking at them. Opening Natalie's car door, he gestured toward the driver's seat. "At thirty-two, I should not have to drag you away from making a public scandal of yourself. Your teen and college years were bad enough. It's a good thing Susan overheard you on the phone telling one of your friends you were going to confront Nicole. I'm making an exception, this time, due to the circumstances even though I warned you not to come up here. Go home or return to my place and have a say-so in the funeral arrangements."

"Your wife has always been nosy." Fisting her hands on her hips, she sought Douglas' help. "Are you really going to side with him and let her get away with killing our brother?"

"I'm siding with Michael right now, agreeing we should move this conversation someplace private. Come on, sis," Douglas cajoled, wrapping an arm around her shoulders. "We were prepared for Tony's death, albeit not this soon or this way."

Douglas, who went through life taking nothing seriously, had been quiet since the police called them together first thing this morning. Maybe too quiet. Michael worried about all his siblings and the family name. So far, he was the only one married with an heir, his son, Jerod, who'd just turned three. Before Tony's medical diagnosis, he'd figured his youngest brother would eventually delegate Nicole to mistress status and marry someone more suitable for the Renaldi name, so he'd left Tony alone.

"Fine, for now. But I *will* confront that bitch, and I can promise you this – she *will* pay for what she's done. Dad taught us all to hunt, and no prey has ever escaped me." Natalie got in her car and shot out of the parking lot with tires screeching.

Michael rubbed the back of his neck then pressed his fob to unlock his car. "If she doesn't show up at my place, call her. She listens to you more than me," he told Douglas over the hood before sliding behind the wheel.

Settling on the passenger side, Douglas replied, "I doubt she'll listen to anyone right now. They were close."

"Yeah, I know." Not only as twins, but there was a ten-year gap between him and his youngest siblings, two separating him and Douglas. Yet he remained closest to his longtime girlfriend, not his wife or brother.

He gave a mental shrug. *It is what it is*, he'd always believed, and wasn't about to change now that he'd reached forty-two. "She needs time, but the arrangements won't wait. We'll handle them, with or without her."

"And what if Nicole is there? Do you want me to talk to her before then?"

Michael started for home, groaning at the thought. Seeing Nicole Wells at the service would be akin to lighting a firecracker under Natalie. "Yes, in a day or two, after everything is finalized. His will won't be read until afterward, but I doubt Tony changed anything. Fred never mentioned him making any changes."

"Fred's an attorney bound by confidentiality first, not friendship."

*****

"True. I'll give him a call, if for no other reason than to be prepared. That news would derail Natalie." Michael didn't need anything else to rile his sister.

"Let's hope Tony knew enough to keep

his holdings in the family." Douglas shook his head, as if befuddled. "I'll never understand how he could be so happy staying home all the time with one woman. That's so contrary to the Renaldi men."

Their father and uncle were never faithful husbands and didn't hide that fact from their sons. If their mother or aunt had known, they never let on, the same with his wife, Susan. "Tony lived his life by a different set of values. I always admired that about him." Michael would miss his little brother. He was the best of them.

*****

Nicole lifted the last box of things she'd left in the bedroom she'd shared with Tony after moving in with her parents six months ago and took one final look around, her heart still aching. She couldn't believe Tony had changed his will and now this was all hers, along with everything else that was in his name only. He never let on about doing that, swearing the Renaldi lawyer to silence until he showed up at the door a day after her hospital dismissal and she was debating where to go from here. She could only imagine the reaction from Michael and Douglas, surprised she hadn't heard from them about it. Natalie remained vocal in the press, claiming she got away with murder, citing the inheritance as motive. Nicole had become numb to her accusations.

"Here, let me help you with that."

Ooops, spoke too soon.

Douglas entered the room and reached for the box, but she stepped aside, irritated and curious all at once. "I've got it, thanks. What are you doing here?" Of the three brothers, he was the best looking with his chestnut hair worn long and curling around his nape and his flirty blue-eyed gaze. She'd never met anyone more conceited.

"Straight and to the point. I admire that." He smiled and ran his fingers down her bare arm.

She didn't move fast enough that time and hated his creepy touch. "That's funny," she stated, heading toward the door. "You wanted nothing to do with me before today.

If you don't mind…"

Blocking her way, he brushed her cheek with his knuckles, his look and voice cajoling as he replied, "Come on, baby, don't be that way. Or are you playing hard to get?"

Nausea churned in Nicole's stomach, and she resisted the urge to kick him. Instead, she stomped out of the room, speaking over her shoulder. "Get out of my house, Doug." Except for Tony, the Renaldis hated it when she called them by the shorter version of their names. But then, Tony hadn't been a pompous ass like Doug.

Without warning, Nicole found her arm in his bruising grip, his cold, contemptuous look replacing his teasing leer. "You may have fooled my little brother, but neither Michael nor I are as gullible. If you want to keep all this"—he spread his free arm out to indicate the spacious house—"I suggest you be as nice to me as you were to Tony."

She tried to pull out of his hold, resisting the urge to tell him the house was already under contract with a Realtor, but he tightened his hand with a scornful laugh. A shiver of unease crept down her spine, his behavior so contrary to his usual indifference toward her, she didn't know how to respond. Luckily, she didn't have to.

"Get your hand off my daughter."

Nicole caught the fleeting surprise in his eyes as Doug dropped his hand and turned to face her father coming up the stairs. "Your daughter, huh? So, you're the one responsible for raising this money-grubbing bitch."

A small smile flitted at the corners of her dad's mouth as he wrapped an arm around her shoulders and they exchanged a quick, conspiring glance. "I couldn't be prouder of my daughter. Now, as she said, get out of her house."

Douglas spun on his heel and stomped down the stairs without a word, his rigid back talking for him.

"I've never seen him like that. People handle grief in different ways. Maybe that's his way." Nicole shrugged, hefting the box in her arms to gain a better hold.

Taking the box from her, Carl Wells said, "Don't make excuses for the likes of him. I should have thrown your charitable intentions in his face. Is this it?"

"Yes, and I'm not just pointing out how uncharacteristic his behavior was." Strolling with him toward the stairs, she added, "I'm glad you didn't mention my plans to give most of the money away." Nicole favored her father with the same black hair and blue eyes, but her penchant for stating her mind in blunt terms came from both her parents. It made for stimulating arguments, especially when her brother came home on leave from the Navy.

When they reached the foyer, he faced her at the door. "You're sure about all this, including moving so far away?"

Nicole smiled to ease the concern reflected on his face. "Yes, and Wyoming isn't all that far. As I said when I bought the property, if it doesn't work out, then I know I'm welcome back here." She stretched up and kissed his cheek then opened the door. "I'll get my purse and be right out."

Grabbing her purse off the staircase newel, Nicole took another sweeping glance of the house where she'd spent so many pleasurable months and said a silent final goodbye. She hoped to find peace and a way to forgive herself for taking Tony's life where she was going. Time would tell if she could.

Chapter Two

His target came into view, sweat rolling down his blackened face as he followed the hooded, long-robed figure with his scoped rifle. Lying on his stomach atop the hillside above the small Afghanistan village, Slade waited for his commander's go-ahead in his earpiece. "Cover your ass by insisting on a direct order confirming your target's identity before taking a shot." He'd learned that from a former military sniper who now trained men to take a life to save others. That last order often soothed the moral battle he waged with himself over his chosen career path. The final attestation of the target's lethal intention to kill as many innocent people as possible was a needed reminder of what a lowlife, deadly degenerate he was about to take out. The many lives saved by one pull of the trigger would ease his conscience until the next assignment when the questions would plague him anew.

A few people emerged from the crude huts and adobe buildings miles away from his perch, the women looking hot in their concealing clothing, some holding the hands of small children. A group of young boys, likely under the age of twelve, kicked a ball around the dirt street, grins creasing their faces. Teens were often recruited or forced to join the war. An old stoop-shouldered man gripping a tall stick for balance shuffled past a donkey grazing in a grassy area. From this distance, they appeared the size of dolls, and only the clothing and uncovered faces told him the gender of the taller boys.

Slade grew itchy the closer his target got to ending those innocent lives, and he prayed for his order to come through, either confirming or denying that was the suicide bomber he was sent to kill. "I'm getting too old for this," he muttered then grunted at thinking twenty-seven was too old for any activity.

A double beep echoed in his ear, the kill

signal he possessed a love-hate relationship with. He pulled the trigger, grateful for the ability to save lives, yet never took one with a gram of salt. Women and children screamed and ran for cover, all except one. She ran straight toward the fallen figure, fell to her knees sobbing, and reaching for the prone would-be bomber. Stunned, Slade pulled out his binoculars and zeroed in on her ravaged face as she turned him over. Bile clogged his throat when he viewed the face of a boy no older than ten, the woman's wails adding to his gut-clenching remorse. The detonation switch to set off the bomb secured to his torso fell from the boy's hand, but confirmation of his intentions didn't matter. Terrorists knew all sorts of ungodly ways to threaten others to do their dirty work, but all he saw was a child dead by his hand.

*****

Slade Kincaid jerked awake and fought to untangle himself from the sweat-dampened sheet. Breathing heavy from reliving his worst nightmare, he got out of bed, not bothering with a light as he reached for his jeans lying at the foot. His Border collie, Chase, rubbed against his leg, and he took a moment to brush a hand over his soft head to let him know he was all right. Wearing nothing but the comfortable worn denim, he padded down the hallway lit by a nightlight, bemoaning his inability to get past that moment in time when he'd taken a child's life. His conscience didn't care about the people his action saved, which included his grieved aunt and cousins. God knows many more children would have perished that day if he hadn't done his job, and the young pawn the terrorists had used had been doomed from the get-go. The boy's relatives in that village had no idea he'd been kidnapped, his parents and siblings threatened with torture and death if he didn't cooperate.

None of that helped when the kid's face snuck by his shield during sleep. Eleven years, and Slade still couldn't forgive himself, or forget. It defied logic, in his mind, but when did logic ever take place fighting a war?

The full moon glowing outside the living area's wide windows guided him into the kitchen, the tile floor cool under his feet compared to the bedroom carpet and hardwood elsewhere. He grabbed a beer from the refrigerator, a dog biscuit for Chase, and made his way out to the back patio through the glass slider in the den. He tossed the treat to Chase, who settled on the patio, content for now. Unable to say the same about himself, he leaned against a post and took a long draw, the cold brew and cool late September air drying his perspiration-damp body. Instead of gunfire resonating in his ears, a baying wolf and the screech of an owl filled the silence of the vast Wyoming countryside.

Slade was the first to build his own home on the ranch he and his brothers had inherited from their father almost two years ago. He'd found some of the peace he craved for his unsettled conscience overseeing the work needed to breed and raise Charbray cattle on a spread of over thirty thousand acres. The crops were another source of income for the ranch, but the bulk of the Kincaid wealth was still pumping the rich oil from the fertile ground. His oldest brother, Brett, handled those and the accounts, thankfully. Slade much preferred the physical labors of running the ranch to the hours needed behind a desk.

He kicked back the last of the beer, set it on the patio table, and picked up his latest carving. Wade Hughes, their dad's foreman, had taught him how to whittle before he'd left for the military, telling him the hobby would come in handy on long, lonely nights away from home. Leaning against the post again, he racked his brain, trying to recall if he'd ever thanked Wade after returning home for good, but couldn't remember. He'd blacked out a lot of that time period he spent trying to cope with guilt even though he knew the boy was doomed the moment he was snatched from his home. After his superiors discovered what the Taliban threatened the youngster with, they told him, but it hadn't mattered to Slade anyway.

By the meager patio light, he could make out the shape of a gnome, a whimsical piece he thought his sister-in-law would like. He would never admit it to his brothers, but he'd enjoyed Brett and Allie's wedding two months ago. The small church in Eagle's Nest was filled to capacity, and even more people attended the reception in Casper that evening. Slade spent most of the time people watching, always a fun way to pass the hours when you weren't big on socializing and crowds.

He'd invited Deb to go with him, mostly to keep the single, eager-to-marry guests away. They used each other that way, which worked well for two people who weren't interested in walking down the matrimony aisle. A frequent play partner at their private club, Deb made the perfect sub in private and was otherwise happy as a clam to maintain a close friendship. Now that Brett was married and Reed, the middle child, had committed to Lily, the pressure would be on him to settle down. Deb had teased him ridiculously about that at the wedding, saying how much she was going to enjoy witnessing his downfall. He let her have her fun, ignoring her and others since he knew the truth – no woman would take on a man who carried such baggage and worked ten to twelve hours a day although he was financially secure.

Besides, he mused with glee, once his brothers started giving their mother the grandchildren she'd been pining for, he would be off the hook. He looked forward to being the cool favorite uncle. Counting his blessings by reminiscing about family always helped to steady him after a bad night. With a twist of his wrist, he started carving the contours on the gnome's hat while the painted streaks of dawn broke on the horizon. Watching a new day unfold with a blend of deep purple and pale pink then brighten to vibrant red, orange, and yellow also helped chase away the dark of night demons.

The sun made its debut, breaking the horizon in a canary-yellow blaze that forced Slade to squint to finish the gnome's hat before returning the wood to the table. The hint of warmth touching his shoulders indicated another day of pleasant weather, something to look forward to with October right around the corner. The first snowfall of the year often hit them by mid-month, which made the end of September a busy time on the ranch. Folding the paring knife, he slipped it into his pocket and went inside to finish dressing and eat something before driving to the barns.

The steel roofs on the two large barns and smaller stable came into view as Slade rounded a corner on the unpaved road that wound through the front portion of their property thirty minutes later. Parking in front of the stable, he spotted the four college kids he had hired last year already loading hay bales to haul to the lower pastures. Their early appearance surprised him. They worked part-time while in school and weren't scheduled until afternoon.

"Morning, boss," Riley called out with a wave before grabbing the two straps wrapped around the bale and hefting it onto the flatbed.

Strolling up to them, Slade nudged his Stetson up and fisted his hands on his hips. "Morning. Now, tell me what gives."

Jeff, the cut-up of the group, flashed a cheeky grin. "We love working here so much we cut class this morning just to help out during this busy time."

Keith sighed and rolled his blue eyes. "Knock it off, Jeff. They canceled classes today, and maybe tomorrow, because of a water line bust."

That, Slade could believe, but it still didn't explain their early clock-in. "And?" He zeroed in on Evan, the one with attitude oozing out of every pore all the time. The only reason he tolerated his insolence was because he knew the signs of emotional baggage, and the kid carried a butt-load of it. "Evan? You never beat around the bush. Let's have it."

"There's a kegger starting around four at the reservoir," he stated with a shrug, his hazel gaze direct, as if defying Slade to lecture them.

"Ah, man, why'd you have to go and tell him that," Jeff whined. Keith and Riley glared at him.

Slade debated his reply. On one hand, he wanted to lecture them, remembering all too well his youth and the lines he and his brothers often skirted when in partying mode. Their father, Casey, left their supervision and discipline up to Wade after their parents' split. When he did spare time in between women for his sons while they spent summers on the ranch, it was all fun and games. Those early college days, however, were a different story, as with most kids.

Dropping his hands, he strode forward and hefted a bale to his shoulder, saying, "My authority begins and ends on this ranch. I'm not your father." For some reason, Evan's shoulders went rigid at that. Ignoring him, Slade swung the bundled hay atop another one. "But I will remind you to be careful, and don't drink and drive. I'll fire your ass if you do. If you need a ride, call me, regardless of the time. You should be able to get two loads out to the feeders this morning."

Reed drove up to the stable and got out of his truck, and Slade lifted a hand to him. "Reed and I will be working out in the fields. You know how to get hold of us." He pivoted, Chase racing ahead as he joined Reed without waiting for a response. "Hey," he greeted his brother.

"Morning. They're early." Reed nodded toward the hands, giving the dog a quick rear rub.

"Canceled classes and a lake party this

afternoon.”

Reed grinned. “Ah, the good old days. I remember them well.”

Slade scoffed as they went into the stable. “Yeah, right. You were already headed toward the straight and narrow your first year when you decided to become a cop.”

“Cops like to party and cut loose. And,” Reed said, opening Apollo’s stall gate, “I’m not a cop anymore.”

“True,” Slade admitted, strolling forward along the wide, concrete aisle separating the two rows of horse stalls. Bandit head-butted him in greeting, the stallion’s black mane sliding along his muscled tan neck. “Hey, boy, ready to ride?”

Reed led Apollo out of the stall holding the reins, eyeing him with a smirk. “If you crooned to the ladies in that voice, they’d fall at your feet.”

“If I wanted a woman to sit at my feet, I’d find one that’s submissive.” He followed Reed out the back way where they tethered the horses at the corral fence and saddled them.

“Speaking of which,” Reed said as he

mounted, "you haven't said if you're coming to the get-together Thursday. We have a few new members."

"I'll try to make it."

Slade thought the three of them were nuts when they decided to buy the old run-down lodge off the highway at auction and renovate into a nightclub. He only agreed because the upper floor was an ideal space for their private BDSM gatherings. Growing up with a wealthy father whose public philandering constantly landed him in the society pages of the Casper paper taught them the benefits of keeping their personal lives quiet. None of them would deny sowing their wild oats when they were younger, but they took commitments seriously and stayed off the gossip party line. They had their mother and stepfather's marriage example to thank for showing them the difference between their parents' views on relationships.

"You need to get out as much as I do after these weeks of putting in long days," Reed stated, interrupting his thoughts.

He wasn't opposed to hanging out at Casey's, the club they'd named after their father, and doing his part in assisting their friend and manager, Jordon Myers. But he was a moody son of a bitch, and he more often than not preferred solitude and quiet to the loud din of a jam-packed room.

"You have Lily now," Slade pointed out. "Why are you pestering me?"

"I don't have to nag her. She's easygoing and sweet, and agrees you should get out more."

"She is that, and you're as whipped as Brett," he returned, scanning the wide-open range for the herd they should be catching sight of any time now.

"Yep, and I love it." Reed pointed to their right. "There they are."

Slade experienced one of those rare twinges of envy at hearing the pleasure in Reed's voice. Almost six months ago, a deranged stalker had set fire to Lily's house in Eagle's Nest with her and Reed inside. His brother's sixth sense and quick actions saved them both and the woman was now incarcerated in a mental facility for violent offenders. Lily's compassion toward the woman who had believed the lies her husband fed her during their affair made it easy to see why his brother had fallen so hard and fast. He adored her and Allie, Brett's wife, but even so, he was content with his life now that he'd learned to live with guilt.

Chase ran ahead, and Reed cast him a quick glance. "Race?"

"You're on." They took off, neck and neck, their mounts eager for the run.

With his stallion's hooves pounding the ground, legs stretching and sides heaving, the wind on Slade's face and sun on his shoulders as he leaned over Bandit's neck, racing his brother, he thought life didn't get better than this.

When Slade called it a day nine hours later, enough daylight still remained to drive home without his headlights. After Reed took off, he checked with the two hands assigned night patrol before heading home himself, pleased they were left with only a small herd to drive close enough to get hay out to them this winter. Turning into his drive, he reached above him to click the garage door opener. He'd debated whether to build the house with the back windows facing the open range or the narrow woods that separated their property from the old Studman place. After spending a good portion of his military days hiding in trees or propped on foliage-covered hillsides, the unobstructed view appealed to him more than the year-round forest greenery.

Slade caught the faint whispering flow of the full creek that ran through the woods, followed by the clearer sharp bark of a nearby dog, as he slid out of the truck. Likely a stray, he thought, shutting the door, then changed his mind when a female voice followed by a whistle filtered through the trees.

"Sam, come!"

The dog must have obeyed because he could barely detect a soft, crooning tone before the more distinct tap of a hammer hitting a nail reached him. Last he heard, the ten acres that lay between the Kincaid ranch and Baily's spread had sold at auction, but that was a few months ago. Curious, and with nothing better to do right now, he put Chase in the house then strode to the path he and his brothers took when running wild in this area. The trail led to the short wooden bridge they'd built themselves to cross the creek when it was too cold to splash in. The wooded area between his place and his neighbor was only about a block wide, and it took him less than ten minutes before he emerged from the trees.

Slade paused to watch the young woman pounding nails into a loose fence board, wondering if anyone else was around. From the looks of it, the entire fence should be replaced instead of repaired, but that was her business. A happy mixed-breed dog ran around the field, chasing something only he could see, or maybe nothing at all. His shaggy black coat was the same color as his owner's chin-length hair that she kept scooping out of her face as she bent over the rail. She was slender, the jeans and high-necked, long-sleeved black tee fitted but not restrictive. The sneakers wouldn't last long if she planned to spend much time in these fields.

He strode forward to introduce himself and lend a hand since no one else had made an appearance. What he did notice was the work that needed to be done on the barn and house, signs the property had stood vacant for many months. She didn't look up as he approached, not even when the dog barked and dashed to hide behind her.

"You're trespassing, in case you didn't notice," she said, dropping a hand to give the dog a quick pet.

The soft voice and caring gesture didn't match the unfriendly tone, and he found himself intrigued. "I'm Slade Kincaid, live right beyond the woods over there." He jerked a thumb behind him.

She sighed and straightened, turning large, sky-blue eyes his way while scraping her hair back. The wispy bangs fell across her forehead again, her wide mouth tightening into a straight line, her face as arresting as her attitude.

"I didn't ask, but I'm tired, so I'll play nice. Nicole Wells, and I live here now."

Amused, Slade decided to push her buttons, just for the heck of it. "I'll help you finish up."

"Why on earth would you do that?" she asked, her voice perplexed, as if she couldn't believe her attitude didn't turn him away.

"Because that's what neighbors do."

She let loose with a rude snort. "Not where I come from."

He read the blue and white lettering on her shirt with the large dog paw print in between the lines. *DOGS MAKE ME HAPPY – YOU NOT SO MUCH*. She had a sense of humor to go with the prickly attitude. He liked that.

"You're in our neighborhood now." To get on her good side, if she had one, he squatted and held his hand out to Sam, who hadn't budged from her legs.

Without taking his eyes off the cowering dog, Slade said, "I assume this is the Sam I heard you calling a few minutes ago."

"Yes, and he doesn't like intruders, either." She whacked another nail with unnecessary force.

"I'm a visitor and friendly neighbor, a far cry from an intruder," he returned. "You'll need another dog if you want to deter intruders."

Sam inched his head around her knee and stretched to sniff his hand. When his long tail thumped the ground, Nicole huffed and muttered, "Traitor."

"Nah, just smart enough to realize I'm no threat." He scratched under Sam's chin then rose and tipped his hat. It was too dark now for her to do much more. "Nice to meet you, Nicole Wells."

Slade barely made out her wry grin. "You too, Slade Kincaid."

*****

Interesting guy.

Nice butt to go with what she could make out of his shadowed jawline, broad shoulders, and deep drawl, the lowered Stetson shielding his gaze, conjuring up all kinds of fantasies.

Nicole shook her head at the fanciful thought as she watched her neighbor walk into the woods. That's what she got for keeping to herself so much this past year and staying holed up on her new property the last two weeks. The first cowboy she talked to sent her mind into the gutter. *He was a diversion from my exhaustion,* she thought, picking up the bag of nails and starting toward the house with Sam at her heels. "You were nicer than I was. What's with that?" she asked him as she held the back door open. Sam trotted inside without answering.

Since setting foot inside her new home and checking out the property she'd purchased through an agent, Nicole had discovered the amount of work needed to get her shelter up and running. She'd kept enough of the money Tony left her to buy this place, turn it into a rescue, and cover the operating expenses. With luck, the contracts she'd signed before leaving Chicago to illustrate children's books would pay her living expenses. Without a mortgage, she wouldn't need much.

A mudroom separated the kitchen from the back door, and she braced a hand on the wall to toe off her shoes, remembering what the neighbor said about boots. She might prefer solitude to socializing for now, but that didn't mean she wouldn't take any advice she could get to make her transition from city life to country girl easier. Bending over, she removed her socks and tossed them into the washing machine on the opposite wall before padding barefoot to the refrigerator.

Scanning her limited options for dinner, Nicole grudgingly admitted she couldn't put off a shopping trip into town much longer. She really missed her mom's home-cooked meals.

Avoiding attention in Chicago, especially from the media with Natalie's prodding, had been impossible after Tony's death and she'd moved in with her parents. They hounded her for interviews, even pestered the volunteers at the shelter once they got wind of her involvement. And after the will was read, Tony shocking everyone, including her, by leaving her everything except his shares in the family company, things got worse and it was easier to stay inside and concentrate on her career as an illustrator.

There were eggs, cheese, and onion enough for an omelet and as she prepared the simple meal, her thoughts drifted to her neighbor. She honestly didn't mind the visit from Slade, but also didn't want to encourage him to stop by whenever the urge struck, even if he was the first man to stir her dormant libido. Nicole had taken a chance on finding the peace and solitude she craved by moving away from the city where she'd spent her whole life. In the last fourteen days, she'd not only found both on this land but the perfect place to start a rescue shelter for dogs. The woods separating her from neighbors were a far cry from the close quarters of apartment living and the compact row of brownstones where her parents lived, both in one of Chicago's poorer and not-so-safe neighborhoods.

There was still quite a bit of adjusting to do in transitioning from city life to country; she'd never expected it to be quick or easy. She filled Sam's food bowl then carried her plate from the rusted stove to the rickety table. Taking a seat in the one chair, she sighed, eyeing her light dinner. While researching the property's location before bidding on the ten acres, she'd learned Casper was the closest big city and second largest in the state after Cheyenne, their combined populations a fraction of Chicago's. After viewing the work needed on the house, barn, and caretaker's cottage the auction website posted, she'd made sure she could get the necessary supplies nearby.

At a minimum of a forty-five-minute drive one way, though, she would have to stock up on frozen groceries that would last for weeks, very different from running into the corner market near her apartment at home every few days. Either that or search for a closer, smaller nearby town where she could pick up essentials that would get her by until she could get into Casper.

Nicole finished the omelet and threw away the paper plate. Unpacking the dishes would wait until she bought a dishwasher, which would have to wait until the kitchen was remodeled. Still hungry, she grabbed a bag of potato chips out of the walk-in pantry, the best feature in the house, and finished it off working a crossword puzzle, curled in the corner of the old, lumpy sofa. She needed to keep her brain occupied so she wouldn't dwell on or fret over the daunting tasks ahead of her. An hour later, she fell asleep in the sleeping bag on top of her bed, a new mattress topping her list, praying she hadn't bitten off more than she could handle.

Chapter Three

Slade was the last to arrive for Sunday brunch at his mother's house the next day. He blamed the new neighbor.

For the first time since he thought he was head over heels in love with Candace Baker in the eighth grade, he couldn't stop thinking about a woman. Nicole Wells carried a chip on her shoulder in a way similar to his attitude after returning home for good from the military. At the time, he'd shoved away family and friends alike, shunning all overtures of support and yearning for nothing more than solitude and enough physical labor to exhaust him. Since meeting Nicole last night, he itched to tell her the work would only go so far in keeping the demons at bay, and he should know. His nights were still haunted by the part he'd played in cutting a child's life short because others were using him as a deadly pawn in the adult game called war.

He arose that morning thinking, why bother; she wouldn't listen any more than he would have ten years ago. His family had refused to give up on him, battling through his defenses and attitude until he caved to their concern and caring and let them back into his life. The age of the last suicide bomber he'd taken out remained his burden alone, but during several nights of imbibing too much alcohol with his brothers, he'd spoken of the toll his military job had taken on him.

Family meant everything to Slade, but when he'd carried his coffee out to the patio this morning, the first thing he heard was the steady strike of a hammer pounding a nail again. Picturing Nicole taking up her daunting task of repairing a fence that should be replaced tempted him to skip brunch, but then he would disappoint his mother. He didn't care for the tug-of-war he'd battled for three hours before finally hopping on his motorcycle and riding into Eagle's Nest. In the last ten years, he hadn't missed a Sunday meal with his mother and stepfather and refused to let one meaningless encounter break that record. If they were more than willing to switch from dinner to brunch to accommodate Allie and Lily's family time when needed, the least he could do was arrive on time. His preoccupation with the new neighbor would have to wait.

Slade could hear voices and laughter from the back yard as soon as he cut the engine and removed his helmet. He hooked the helmet on the handlebars, combed his fingers through his hair to get the longer strands off his face and neck, and then followed the paved walk around the side to the wrought iron gate. The smokey scent of charcoal hit him as he walked into the back yard and saw his brothers and parents gathered. The cool breeze sent smoke spiraling away from the covered patio, chilly enough for Allie and Lily to wear long sleeves.

"There you are." Andrea Hastings, his mother, rushed forward to greet him, appearing closer to forty instead of already turning sixty with her wide smile and sparkling green eyes. Going on her toes, she kissed his cheek. "Come on. William is cooking German sausages, and I made German potato salad."

"Sounds good."

It would sound even more appealing if Slade didn't think of Nicole at that moment and wonder if she was eating alone today. None of his business, and shouldn't bug him, he reminded himself, following his mom toward food and family. Before Reed retired from law enforcement and Brett moved back home from San Antonio, he'd spent many days with the hired hands, preferring solitary meals over seeking company. During the week, he still ate alone, so no big deal.

Brett handed him a glass of iced tea, his shirt sleeves rolled up to reveal forearms as tan as Slade's from working outdoors. "Sorry I couldn't get out there yesterday to help you and Reed. Lily called me with a domestic abuse case."

"I was at the shelter when the young woman came in," Allie stated, joining them. "The poor girl was really shook up." She gave him a quick hug, which he returned.

Lily, and now Allie, volunteered at

Casper's homeless shelter. Unfortunately, there was no shortage of men with tempers and the people they claimed to care about bearing the brunt. Lucky for those victims, Brett offered free legal services which sometimes called for putting in weekend hours.

"No problem," Slade told Brett as Allie moved to her husband's side and leaned against him. "We had enough help. The guys got it done."

"Not without complaining," Reed put in from the grill. "These are about done, right, William?"

Their stepfather nodded, his wide chef's hat tilting. A knee-length white apron with *Chef Will* in red lettering completed the ensemble he wore whenever he did the cooking. "Another minute or two." He glanced at Lily and Andrea sitting at the table. "Go ahead and get the potatoes out of the oven, hon. Then we'll be in."

"I'll help."

Lily patted Slade's shoulder as she followed his mother inside, Allie turning to go with them. She was more reserved than

Allie, yet both women were perfect matches for his older brothers. He was reaping more than one benefit by welcoming them into the family.

While they ate, talk around the table bounced from topic to topic, most of which he listened to more than participating. Sinking his teeth into a sauerkraut-covered sausage slathered with mustard, his thoughts again drifted to Nicole, pondering on whether she would take a break from work or not. Why should he worry if she pushed herself? Damn it, he wasn't her keeper; he'd barely met the woman. Her input in their short conversation consisted of telling him to go away. She'd made it clear she didn't want help and preferred to be left alone, so why was he itching to do the opposite and go bug the crap out of her?

Slade jolted when Allie waved a hand in front of his face. "Earth to Slade. Pass the carrots, please." Her curious look wasn't the only one.

"Sorry. Daydreaming." He handed her the bowl of chopped carrots glistening with caramelization.

"Duh." Across the table, Reed raised a brow and rested an arm atop Lily's chair beside him. "Anything you want to share?"

Might as well, he mused. The idea that popped into his head would require enlisting their help if he went through with it. "I met the new neighbor. She bought the Studman farm. From our brief conversation, she appeared to be tackling the repairs needed for an animal rescue by herself." He shrugged, hoping the gesture conveyed this was no big deal when he asked, "Anyone want to help me haul some lumber over and help put up a new fence?"

His mother and Allie beamed at him and replied at the same time. "She?"

"You never get involved with neighbors," Brett stated.

Slade glared at the three of them. "It's only a short fence, and we have plenty of wood slats, so don't make anything more of it than a few hours of neighborly help. Are you in or not?" he asked his brothers.

"I am," Reed said. "Lily's brother won't be in until this evening."

"Yes. Levi texted and said it would be

around seven. I appreciate you changing dinner to earlier, today, Andrea, so I can be home when he arrives."

"Not a problem, Lily, dear. I think that's a wonderful idea, Slade." She sent Brett a pointed look.

"Yes, of course I'll help," he answered as Allie stood to gather plates with Lily.

"If you have time, Lily, we can run over some sandwiches later. I'd like to meet… what's her name?"

He rose and narrowed his eyes at Allie. "Don't even think about pulling any matchmaking stunts."

Smiling, she quipped, "I won't. Just following your example and making a neighborly visit, that's all."

As she and Lily carried dishes into the kitchen, he turned to Brett. "Keep an eye on her." Allie had good intentions, but he still didn't want her butting into his personal life.

"I always do," he replied with amusement.

*****

Slade arrived at their storage barn before his brothers, who were dropping off Lily and Allie first, and he backed up to the wide sliding doors to make it easier and faster to hook up the flatbed. With around four hours of daylight left to work outside, they should get a majority of the fence enclosing half an acre behind Nicole's house replaced. If she balked at accepting their help, he could always point out how much work she faced building a shelter, he mused, sliding out to open up the doors.

Brett finished backing into the barn close enough to attach the flatbed, Reed riding with him. "So, you've already met the new neighbor," he stated, reaching for his hat sitting on the dash before shutting his truck door.

Reed strolled up to Slade, grinning, and clapped him on the shoulder. "We're trying to figure out how that happened. Being the least sociable, you didn't piss her off already, did you?"

"Not yet, but there's time. She has an attitude to rival mine and won't be happy to see us." Slade jerked his head toward the open barn. "Shall we?"

"Then why are we doing this?" Brett asked, following him inside.

Slade pulled his work gloves from his belt and put them on then bent to attach the trailer to the back of his truck. "Because she's attempting to shore up a fence that's too rotted with age to make it worth the time and effort."

Reed hefted a stack of boards from the stash along the side, grunting. "Will she welcome our help or boot us off her property?"

"She won't welcome us, and she'll likely try to get us to go," he replied, filling his arms with lumber.

Brett followed and lowered his load onto the trailer. "She must have made quite an impression to get you to return of your own volition. I like her already."

"Don't make more out of this than a friendly gesture from neighbors."

He returned inside to get another load, ignoring his brother's laughter. It was easier to let them think what they wanted than to argue. Besides, he couldn't help admiring

Nicole's grit and determination in taking on the large project of opening a shelter without seeking help. Maybe a little assistance here and there would keep her from burning out sooner rather than later.

That was Slade's one and only intention for returning to the new neighbor's place today.

*****

Nicole glanced out the open kitchen window, swallowing the last bite of a peanut butter sandwich. There were different sounds in the countryside where woods surrounded by wide-open spaces replaced concrete and skyrises and Mother Nature's song whispered in the breeze carrying the rustle of leaves and the trill of birds. She was still acclimating to several vast differences from what she'd grown up with in the city, but the work and challenges ahead of her were what she needed. *Speaking of which.* She stood and tossed the napkin then returned outside, reminding herself the work wouldn't get done by itself. The cement slab around the back step would never pass as a patio, but there were more urgent replacements and repairs that required attention first.

She trekked across the ill-kept lawn, pulling on the too-large work gloves she'd found in the old barn that required the most renovation. The crunch of large tires rolling up the dirt and gravel drive drew her thoughts away from the contractor's scheduled visit tomorrow. A shamrock-green oversized truck towing a flatbed trailer loaded with boards parked alongside the Subaru Forester she had traded her compact car in on before driving to Wyoming. Nicole's disgruntlement at the interruption failed to prevent a hitch in her pulse when she recognized Slade Kincaid emerging from behind the wheel. She didn't care for that reaction any more than she did for his and the other two men's unannounced arrival, and moved at a brisk pace to find out what he was doing.

Nicole tried hard not to appreciate the better, daylight view of Slade's broad chest in a worn work shirt, his rippling forearms exposed from the rolled-up sleeves, and bristled profile beneath the lowered Stetson. *Okay, there's something about the whole rugged-cowboy package that has an appeal city dwellers lack.* That didn't mean she wanted his company any more today than last night. She untucked her hair from behind her ears to ensure it covered her neck scar before talking to them.

Slade faced her as she reached the truck, tilting his head toward her fisted hands going to her hips. "You'll find gloves and boots in your size at Ina's mercantile off the highway heading north," he said by way of a greeting. "Nicole Wells, these are my brothers, Brett and Reed."

She gave the two men a quick nod but, before either could respond, she confronted Slade. "Why are you here?"

Turning his back to her, he followed his brothers and started loosening the straps holding the boards, talking over his shoulder. "You need a new fence. What you're doing won't hold up."

Nicole tried not to fume simply because he was right. The wood they brought appeared much sturdier than the weather-worn flimsiness of her fence. She caved, somewhat. "Fine," she bit out with grudging concession, picking up a heavy box of nails for something to do. "I appreciate the gesture, but ask next time. You're better off driving closer to the fence. It's not as if you'll hurt the yard before you reach the field." Turning her back on the three men, she led the way across the overgrown yard, keeping her face averted from the paint job the house needed.

The truck rumbled past her, and Nicole went right to work alongside them a minute later, helping Slade move the old boards out of the way.

"This place sat neglected for way too long," Brett commented, pounding on the thick post Reed was holding steady. "I can get you a good contractor, Nicole."

"Jim Baker is coming by tomorrow."

Slade nodded. "He's good, and he won't rob you blind. Hey, Sam." He scratched behind his ears, and Sam was in heaven.

Nicole gave her dog the evil eye for getting friendly with Slade. The man didn't need an incentive to return. "Go chase rabbits, Sam," she grumbled, yanking on a stubborn slat.

"Get over your snit before you hurt yourself." Slade jerked the board off and tossed it on the pile, his jaw taut.

She returned his glare, noticing his eyes were slate gray. "You're the one who arrived uninvited and unannounced. Read it and believe it." She pointed to the saying in white lettering on her navy, long-sleeved top, *All I care about is dogs – And maybe 2 people.* His lips quirked, as if he couldn't help himself, his brothers gazing over with curiosity. Nicole swore the heat suffusing her face was not due to three pairs of male eyes ogling her chest at her invitation.

"That leaves you out, Slade. Everyone likes me and Brett," Reed drawled.

"Bite me. You." He pointed his hammer at Nicole. "Learn to accept a friendly offer of assistance around these parts and the fact your dog likes me. Back to work."

Finding it hard to argue with that, she nodded and worked alongside him in silence for over an hour and a half, amazed at the progress the four of them made in that short time. The old fence sat in a pile a few feet from the new fencing enclosing about 70 percent of the area she allotted for the larger rescue dogs to run around. The last section would attach to the barn side where all she would have to do is open that door then release a few from their kennels at a time. The sun had reached its highest peak and warmth, and now the temperature would drop much faster than it rose, so it surprised her when Brett suggested they keep going until finished.

"You've done plenty, and I appreciate it, and how much you've accomplished. Go ahead and enjoy what's left of your Sunday with your families." The last thing she needed was more guilt poking at her conscience.

Brett squeezed her shoulder and handed her another slat. "We're good. Our girls will be along soon with something to eat, and we should have this finished by then."

"They don't need to do that. Go home in time for your dinner," she insisted.

Nicole didn't care for the idea of more visitors any more than she did the fleeting twinge in her abdomen when she imagined what type of woman Slade had chosen. While she could appreciate good looks paired with a hot body, curiosity about his love life didn't sit well with her. Her interest in men died with Tony, and her healthy sex drive had lain dormant since his diagnosis over eight months ago. With all the work ahead of her, the last thing she wanted was for hormones to kick back into gear.

A wide grin creased Slade's tanned, whiskered cheeks, and she was taken aback by the humor lacing his voice as he stated, "When Allie sets her cap on doing something, there's no dissuading her, but hey, go ahead and tell her that when she and Lily get here."

Reed hammered a board in place but glanced at Nicole. "My Lily is sweet and biddable. She wants to say hello though."

Why did a few words have to make her sound like such a shrew? And were women still called shrews? Her arms ached, and she was tired. That must be the reason for such inane thoughts.

"Your Lily is only sweet and biddable when she's not being stalked by a deranged sociopath," Brett stated around the nail clenched between his teeth.

They said enough to pique her curiosity about both women but not to the extent she wouldn't rather finish and everyone leave. She would force herself to be nice though.

As if reading her thoughts, Slade bent down, his warm breath fanning her earlobe when he whispered, "If I can hang around, you can suck it up."

Nicole nodded, ignoring the shiver ghosting down her spine, noticing no one mentioned a third woman. Since she wasn't about to ask, she focused on completing the fence.

*****

Allie and Lily arrived just as Nicole left the guys to finish stacking the old wood close enough she could get to it for firewood. She didn't risk mentioning her lack of experience with wood-burning fireplaces in case they used that as another reason to visit. Looking out the front window, she spotted a vehicle coming up the drive and parking behind the trailer. It was a good thing the narrow road from the highway to the house was long enough, she mused. With the fence finished, she could scratch one big chore off her list, and that put her in a much better frame of mind concerning unexpected guests. At least for today.

Nicole opened the door for the blonde and the brunette, each carrying a tote. One or both emitted a hunger-inducing aroma.

The blonde sporting one purple streak in her hair held up her carrying case. "I hope you like pulled pork. I'm Allie Kincaid, Brett's wife."

"And I'm Lily Regan, going to be Reed's wife next spring. This"—she held up her contribution—"is Ina's cheesy potato casserole but my homemade cookies."

Stepping back, she gestured for them to come in, finding it hard not to appreciate them for the food alone. She hadn't realized how tired her taste buds were of slapped-together sandwiches. "Nicole Wells, and I appreciate the food as much as your guys' help this afternoon." What the house lacked in upkeep, it made up for with space. The online pictures hadn't done justice to the large rooms, and she pointed toward the dining area off the kitchen where her table opened long enough to seat eight comfortably. She'd adjusted to the extra space inside much quicker than all those empty acres surrounding her. "The place is outdated, but I can vouch for its cleanliness."

"It'll be awesome once it's restored. The woodwork is beautiful," Lily stated, setting her tote on the table next to Allie's.

"If you want help, we're good at rolling up our sleeves and pitching in." Allie flipped her a cheeky grin. "We'll even give you advanced notice before we come over."

Nicole narrowed her eyes and laid the paper plates in front of the chairs as the guys were entering the mudroom and might hear. "Did Slade say something about my attitude?"

"Don't worry. We got a kick out of it, considering how unsociable he can be at times."

"Your wife is talking about me again, Brett." Slade didn't hesitate to take a seat and reach for the steaming potatoes. "You've got to try the Hendersons' restaurant, Nicole. Sit down."

She took a seat where she was, next to

Slade. the opposite end of the chair next to his he'd pulled out. Everyone except Slade grinned as they sat down, Allie saying, "Oh, I do like you, Nicole."

Ignoring that, she scooped pulled pork onto her plate then addressed Slade. "Only if it's close to a grocery store. That's priority one tomorrow after the contractor leaves."

Reed took the dish from her. "You're in luck, then. Ina and Howard own the closest shopping option, right next to their diner. The mercantile carries everything, including groceries."

Her gaze flicked down the table. "Slade mentioned a mercantile not too far. Thanks."

Turning her attention to eating, she listened to them talk, nodding or replying with a "thanks" when someone would offer a suggestion, but otherwise staying quiet. Sam had dashed into the bedroom upon seeing the crowd inside, and she couldn't blame him. The table no longer appeared spacious with three large men taking up so much room, and they were both used to a quiet living environment. In Chicago, her apartment, Tony's house, and her parents' place had been her refuges from noise and people after a day spent going from campus to working part-time at the downtown bookstore managing the children's section then stopping by the shelter.

Nicole breathed a sigh of relief when Lily stood, picking up a few empty plates, and announced, "We have to go. Nicole, both Allie and I work a lot from home now and can go to lunch with you, if you'd like. My brother is passing through tonight and will stay tomorrow, but any other day this week will work for me. How about you, Allie?"

"I'm available. How about Wednesday?"

"Can I let you know? I appreciate the invite, but and a lot depends on what the contractor says tomorrow. I have deliveries scheduled for the end of the week." All of which was true, so she didn't care about Slade's skeptical look, even if she was happy to see them leaving.

Of course, Slade would have to be the last to walk out, pausing on the threshold when he donned his hat. The others were out of earshot as he leaned in, his wide shoulders and big body filling the doorway.

"I left a card on the kitchen counter with my number to add when you put in Allie's and Lily's." He pinched her chin, his low, deep tone slithering through her like hot lava. "Be nice. Give them a call and yourself a break." With a tilt of his Stetson, he pivoted and left.

Refusing to stand there and ogle his sexy, loose-limbed stride from the back, she closed the door and leaned against it, fanning herself instead. Her chin tickled from the press of his calloused thumb, her blood flowing with a warm surge that pooled between her legs, leaving her damp. Nicole couldn't recall when, if ever, she'd experienced such an intense, heated reaction to a man's nearness while still clothed. He wasn't even her type, but nonetheless, she vowed not to let a case of lust detract her from her goals.

Chapter Four

Renaldi Mansion, Chicago

Natalie slammed the cut-crystal glass down on the bar top, whiskey splashing onto her hand. "I'm not letting her get away with it, I don't care where she went to hide out. Who the hell wants to live in Wyoming?"

"Sit down, Natalie. I find your constant tantrums tiresome." Michael, standing behind the bar in the corner of his great room, took the glass, and set it out of reach.

Bending his head, he pressed his thumb and forefinger between his eyes, hoping to ward off the headache brewing. She'd been going on for thirty minutes and driving him nuts since she and Douglas arrived for

Sunday dinner. Thank God both of them had moved out of their parents' home within a year of him inheriting the mansion. Even with over eight thousand square feet to spread out in, Natalie's spoiled attitude and Douglas' irresponsible ways managed to intrude on his life. As long as they did their jobs with the company and stayed out of the tabloids, he left them alone. On Friday, Natalie had refused to tone down her tirade after learning Nicole Wells had relocated to Wyoming, too far out of his sister's reach to continue her ongoing harassment of the woman. He'd booted her out of his office, hoping that would put an end to it.

No such luck.

"She's just letting off steam. Let her get it over with so we can dine in peace."

He glared at Douglas who was perched on a stool wearing one of his relaxed, *who gives a shit* grins. "She's been letting off steam all weekend. Enough is enough." Michael directed that order to both of his annoying siblings.

"Not until you do something about her," Natalie snapped, taking up a mutinous stance with her arms crossed, her shoulders stiff.

Throwing up his arms, he demanded, "What do you think I can do? She defended herself against Tony's attack. There's no refuting that. The only thing you accomplished by stalking her these past months was to make a public spectacle of yourself and send her packing. I'm ordering you now to let it go and quit dragging our name through the mud."

In answer, she stomped over to the sofa and snatched her purse. Her heels clicked on the tile entry floor before she yelled back, "Obviously, I loved Tony more than you."

The door slammed, her jab cutting Michael to the quick. He picked up her glass and finished the contents in one burning swallow.

"Don't take that to heart," Douglas said, his gaze compassionate for once. "They shared a bond as twins, and being the only girl and the baby to boot, she's been impossible since the terrible twos."

"Which everyone, including you and I, made concessions for way too long." He blew out a breath, wishing yet again he had fought harder to bring his youngest brother home after his diagnosis. "Tony was the best of us." Regrets wouldn't change anything, however, and he shoved aside the painful loss to focus on the living. "I won't lose Natalie also, and at the rate she's going, she'll land her ass in jail, so I'll do what's necessary to stop her. Come on. Just because she chose to skip Andre's shrimp tartare doesn't mean we will."

"Her loss, and more for us."

Michael followed Douglas, his eyes shifting toward the French doors and sweeping view of the green, landscaped acres behind the house, taking in the shimmering, Olympic-size pool and thousand-square-foot pool house. He controlled a multibillion-dollar company and his personal wealth afforded him anything money could buy, yet he couldn't save his brother, and so far, he'd failed to divert his sister from the self-destructive path she was on.

Health issues were beyond his means, but one way or another, he vowed, Michael would not allow Natalie to destroy her future or continue to link the family name to scandal.

✶✶✶✶✶

Natalie fumed all the way home. She thought the heart-wrenching shock of her beloved brother's terminal diagnosis was the worst news she could hear, but that was nothing compared to learning *that woman* had killed him. He was supposed to pass away gently, surrounded by those who loved him, not gunned down in his own home by a money-hungry whore. Her eyes filled with tears as she recalled Tony's teasing. *Face it, sis. It doesn't matter who I go out with, she won't be good enough for your approval.* And he was right.

Michael either didn't understand the special connection she shared with her twin or didn't care about how he died, but she did. And one way or another, she swore *that woman* would not know a moment's peace regardless of where she lived.

✶✶✶✶✶

Douglas called Natalie as soon as he left Michael's house. His resentment of Nicole's scornful rebuff had festered these past months, and he'd silently cheered his sister on when she would publicly lay into her. However, he was better off keeping his desire to side with Natalie from Michael, who took his position as head of the Renaldi family seriously.

The only other part of life he focused on with such unbending purpose was sex. Women did not turn him down. Ever. Call it ego, spoiled, or lucky, it was all the same to him. That nasty altercation was not only a first but from a nobody. Some things he couldn't let stand. How many could claim they'd caught the interest of two Renaldi brothers? None he knew of. Instead of the gratitude he expected, she'd turned on him in disgust.

The humiliating set down from her father didn't bear rehashing. His only saving grace was no one other than those two knew what happened that day. The pleasure of Nicole's departure didn't mitigate his need for payback though.

"If you're calling to side with Michael, I don't want to hear it," Natalie answered as Douglas pulled up at a stop sign.

"Relax, brat. I'm on my way. Two heads are better than one when plotting revenge." Douglas hung up with a smile.

*****

The contractor arrived two hours late then made up for it by spending three hours checking out the house, caretaker's cottage, and barn, making detailed notes on repairs. Leaning on her elbows braced on the kitchen counter, Nicole glanced at the list and estimated price tag, rather surprised it wasn't higher. She'd donated the proceeds from selling Tony's house to various charities, but about half of what he left her remained in a savings account in Chicago. She'd kept enough to stay out of debt buying the property and covering the expenses of repairs, putting in five indoor/ outdoor kennels, updating and furnishing the house and cottage, and saving some for the rescued dogs' vet and food expenses. The home inspector had assured her both living quarters were solid, with updated plumbing and electric, and only needed a cosmetic facelift, which helped her finances.

Glancing up, she nodded at Jim who stood across from her, finishing a glass of iced tea. "Okay. Slade Kincaid vouched for you, and this looks good. When can you start?"

"I can get a construction crew out here in about ten days. Maybe a little sooner if a smaller job gets finished by the end of the week. In the meantime, I'll order supplies and give your preferences for the house and cottage interior redos to my interior design assistant who will call you." He jerked a thumb out the window. "The Kincaids are good people. Did Slade build the fence for you?"

She normally didn't care for bragging, but, darn it, she'd also worked long and hard on it. "Along with his brothers and myself."

Lucky for him, he didn't appear surprised or even impressed. Setting the glass down, he picked up his hat and said, "Feel free to stack anything you don't want from the barn and cottage in a burn pile, anywhere out in the open, away from the woods. I'll call you with a more definitive time schedule."

"Thanks," she replied, walking out with him.

Sam came trotting out from the bedroom as soon as the door closed. With tail wagging, all happy now that the stranger had left, he nudged her hand for attention.

"What's with you? Jim is a nice man, yet you run off without even checking him out. And this is after you cozy up to Slade, who's bigger, gruffer, and well, annoying." All true, which didn't explain why every time he popped into her head, she grew warm in places that had no business getting hot and bothered over the man.

"He is *so* not my type," she told her dog with a final scratch behind his ears. "You better learn to like Jim. You'll be seeing a lot more of him than the neighbor soon. Come on. Let's go for a walk."

Nicole had planned on checking out the mercantile this afternoon, but one glance at the clock and she decided to wait until morning. There was still enough daylight left to find the place, but she didn't relish driving the long stretch of unfamiliar highway in the dark. At home, there was always traffic, day and night, to light up the roads, and no wild animals darting out of nowhere. She was still acclimating to the odd howling, hooting, and screeching night sounds that were either calming or nerve-wracking as opposed to the ruckus from neighbors on the other side of her walls.

Taking advantage of the last hour or so of daylight, she and Sam explored more of the property, believing Tony would approve what she was trying to do here. He'd been crazy about Sam and had accompanied her to donate time at the shelter, always insisting on loading up with food and toys for both dogs and cats. They strolled by the barn, and she looked around for the two stray cats who, so far, had resisted all efforts to allow her close. She figured they kept the mice under control, but put out food and clean water anyway, hoping they would learn to trust her.

They came across a narrow trail veering into the woods around the same area where she'd first seen Slade. Peering through the dense trees, she couldn't glimpse a house or barn but was close enough to hear the gurgling stream. Another day, she would take Sam down to the water where he would love to splash and romp, not because she was curious how close Slade he was. Not that she would admit anyway.

"Come on, boy. Let's head back and find something to eat." All this outdoor exercise had stirred up her appetite, and the air had turned cooler with the sun dipping.

The next day didn't go as planned, either. The designer, Taylor Schmidt, brought out a van full of samples, from flooring to counters and catalogs to browse, which took hours. They walked through the house making choices, then the small cottage, taking a break to eat the fresh muffins Taylor had picked up from a bakery in Eagle's Nest on her way here from Casper. With her head swimming with colors and textures, Nicole spent what was left of that afternoon drawing for one of her children's books contracts, her dream job both fun and soothing.

Allie called first thing Wednesday

morning to ask about lunch, and, since that fit into her plans, Nicole agreed to meet them at the restaurant. All her plans in initiating this move had been centered around the need for solitude, an ache that intensified every time the press found and hounded her for an interview or Natalie showed up at the shelter or work to harass her. She enjoyed the girls' company, but all she wanted today was to show her appreciation for their thoughtfulness the other day by accepting their invitation.

Sam didn't look happy when she left, but he'd enjoyed a long romp that morning while she flagged the area to fence in behind the house for a large yard. He always obeyed her, coming as soon as she called to him, even if he was chasing a rabbit or squirrel, but she would never leave him unattended outside. There was no telling what he would do with her gone.

The shopping center was about half a mile off the highway but easy to spot by the crowded parking lot. Nicole found a place in the middle, close to the mercantile which sat between the restaurant and a small laundromat. She would have brought a load had she known about it as her washer and dryer wouldn't arrive for another week. She walked toward the restaurant thinking she should have thought this move through more thoroughly. She'd spent more time and effort getting acclimated to her new environment and making preparations to take in needy dogs than mourning Tony's death and her hand in ending his life.

The two sessions with a grief counselor her parents had suggested were not much help. The guilt still lingered, just under the surface, and with it the unanswerable question – had there been another option? She realized the futility of asking that, but for that reason alone, she could look at her scars and be grateful for the reminder of how far gone he had been in those final moments.

Nicole heard her name and glanced toward the door, seeing Lily waving. Shoving off the past, she focused again on the here and now, returning her greeting. "Hi. Sorry, my head was in the clouds. *Oh*, what smells so good?" she asked as they entered and the aroma of fresh-baked goods hit her.

"*Mmm*, Ina's baking. Pies and bread, her specialties. That's her behind the counter." She returned the older woman's wave. "Her husband, Howard, is one of the cooks. We're over here."

"Popular place," she commented, eyeing the row of customers seated at the long counter and the number of occupied tables. A tall pie stand loaded with decadent desserts sat next to the register, tempting people to add one to their tab.

"It is, with good reason."

The ends of Lily's mahogany hair swung around her upper back as Nicole followed her through the filled tables to a corner where Allie waited. Each of the blonde's white nails sported a fall icon — leaves, pumpkins, witches, turkeys — that covered the upcoming holidays.

"I love your jewelry and nails," Nicole told her, taking a seat. "But with all the work I have to do, it's best to stay Plain Jane." She held up her bare nails and wiggled her fingers.

Lily grinned. "She's tried to talk me into going with her to get mine done. I prefer clear polish."

"Boring." Allie rolled her eyes, handing a menu to Nicole. "Everything is good. I'm having the chicken melt. Save room for pie."

"There's always room for pie, but that bread smells too good to pass up. I'll order some to take home. All this fresh air and the physical labor I'm not used to sure keeps the appetite stirred up."

"What are you used to?" Lily asked, setting aside the menu and reaching for her water glass.

Nicole waited until the waitress took their orders before replying. "The big city. Crowds, traffic, constant noise, and stuffy air unless the wind is gusting. Once I get a few dogs, it will be nice keeping them outside for a while each day without having to walk them. But I could use help with hiring a handyman who likes dogs."

"I'm glad you asked, and, if you're open to giving second chances, I may have someone for you."

Seeing the guarded but hopeful look on Lily's face made her think the person she had in mind was someone from the shelter.

Treading cautiously, she replied, "I'm open to hearing about who you have in mind as long as you've considered my isolation. I don't want to be put in the position of defending myself against an employee, regardless of his past difficulties or present circumstances." That sounded self-centered and cold, even to her, but she stifled the urge to reveal her scars and explain herself.

She breathed easier when Lily nodded and said, "Absolutely, and there aren't many I would recommend from the shelter right now. Mental illness plagues most of the homeless. Paul couldn't cope with the tragic loss of his family ten years ago and ended up losing his job then his home. He's been trying to find his way back and a purpose in life ever since. I've seen the longing on his face when others bring their pets in, and he's a good handyman, from the work he's done around the shelter."

They paused the conversation when their food came, and Nicole dug in to her sandwich, thinking about Lily's recommendation. She struggled with the death of one person and couldn't imagine the pain of losing a family.

Empathizing with someone's hardships, though, didn't mean she should take a chance on hiring someone with obvious mental issues. She'd taken a risk staying so long with Tony, praying for more time after he began showing swift, uncharacteristic mood changes and deteriorating cognitive awareness.

Nicole noted the expectation on both their faces. "I'll talk to him, but I have to be honest." She paused, weighing how much to tell them. Her scars were covered by her high-collared pullover, but eventually she would have to wear something that couldn't hide them. Instead of revealing the whole story today, though, she would say enough to explain her hesitancy. "Someone I knew very well, trusted with my life, became ill and turned on me. Not his fault, none of it, but the scars are there and still hard to deal with. I don't want to put myself in that position again."

"I'm so sorry," Allie replied first, her blue gaze compassionate.

"Me too. I worked on getting Paul to open up to me for three months, and, when he did, I saw the man he used to be when he had a wife, baby daughter, and two-year-old son to come home to every day. He worked in bank security, but that was a decade ago."

Lily's tone held a wealth of compassion, and Nicole wasn't so jaded she couldn't sympathize with the man's loss. "When the cottage is ready, I'll call, and we'll go from there."

"If you're planning on just dogs, it shouldn't be hard to get a referral from the shelter in Casper if Lily's guy doesn't work out," Allie suggested as they resumed eating.

"I've talked to them, and I'm going to kennel their overflow, along with a few strays I come across. I don't want people dumping unwanted pets on my doorstep all the time, so I'm not advertising or naming the shelter. I'd like to own a horse someday, but otherwise I only want dogs. Adding cats would be too much," she answered, nibbling on a fry.

Lily smiled at her. "I pegged you as more of a city girl."

"Trust me, I am."

Allie raised a slim brow. "But you know how to care for a horse?"

She shrugged and reached for her tea. "Not a clue."

"Ever ridden?" Lily asked.

"Nope, but I'll learn. I've got time." Lots of time and obligations only to the animals she would take in. That was what Nicole needed right now.

"Slade..."

Holding up her hand to stop Allie's suggestion, she shook her head. "No Slade anything. That that man rubs me the wrong way. Don't get me wrong; the whole sexy-cowboy package can get any woman's blood pumping. Opposites attract, and, from what I can tell, our personalities are too similar to get along."

Lily chuckled. "Heard you had an attitude."

"Serves my brother-in-law right to deal with someone just like him. But, hey, lust is always fun for a while. Those guys can get creative, including on horseback," Allie said.

Her traitorous body responded with damp heat at the image Allie's comment conjured. She tried erasing it, but it wouldn't disappear until the waitress arrived with their tickets. Pushing her plate away, she thanked her and stood. "I have a lot of shopping to do. Thanks for the invitation. Lily, I'll get back to you in a few weeks."

They walked up to the register with her, Allie leaning close to whisper, "Something to think about."

She didn't elaborate, leaving Nicole to wonder whether she meant asking Slade to help her ride or going for the lust, or both.

"You've brought me a new customer." Ina smiled at them and held her hand out to Nicole. "Ina Henderson. Thanks for coming in. How was everything?"

"Nicole Wells, and excellent, thank you. I would top it off by taking that Boston cream pie with me, but I have a long list of shopping next door before I head home."

Ina rang them up, saying, "I'll set it aside, box it up, and you can grab it when you're done. On the house. You bought Studman's place."

"Word spreads fast around here." Another thing to adjust to, she thought, preferring the anonymity of city life.

"Ina hears all and knows all," Allie

quipped, giving the woman a fond smile. "I ought to know. She's my mom's best friend."

"That's right. For instance, I can tell you, Nicole, your neighbors are good people. You need anything, don't hesitate to ask them."

"I keep hearing that," she murmured. "Thanks for the pie. I'll be back shortly."

Nicole said goodbye to Allie and Lily before strolling down to the mercantile, searching her memory banks for a time when the proprietor at any eatery she'd visited in Chicago offered a freebie as a friendly gesture. She drew a blank and put Ina's as a perk in the positive column for when she found herself questioning this drastic move or a place to go when her self-imposed isolation got to her. To be honest, she'd enjoyed lunch with the neighbor girls more than she'd thought, and went ahead and added them to that list.

The center mercantile stretched wide and long, and it took her over an hour to fill a cart with groceries and necessities she hadn't brought with her. She refused to admit Slade's suggestion was the reason she purchased the low-heeled ankle boots. Where that man was concerned, denial would stay her middle name.

She took advantage of the polite hired help to load her vehicle then returned for the pie. "I appreciate the offer, Ina, but I'm more than happy to pay for it. Lily said you bake from scratch, which is a lot of work."

"Work I love, so never you mind. It's always a pleasure to welcome new neighbors. Stop by Casey's on a Friday or Saturday night sometime. That's a popular gathering place just north of here where you'll meet a lot of locals your age. You can't miss the lighted parking from the road."

Nicole took the pie, her mouth watering for a piece despite not being hungry after that big lunch. "I'll keep that in mind, and thanks again. I'm sure I'll become a regular here in no time."

"Then I'll see you soon," Ina returned, with a twinkle in her eyes behind the wire-rimmed glasses.

Nicole welcomed the warm fuzzy filling her as she returned to her SUV, taking it as proof it wasn't just the annoying, libido-stirring neighbor who could cause such a reaction around here.

Chapter Five

Slade shifted in the saddle, eyeing the large herd of Charbrays grazing around a big lake., the midafternoon sun warm enough to still get by without a burdensome coat. A sense of proud accomplishment always spread through him when he saw so many of the hardy, hefty breed, a lot of them showing the bulge of calf bearing. This particular breed's foraging attributes and sheer robustness enabled them to endure the cold winters. Their father had started raising the Australian breed with coats ranging from light red to cream after making millions off the oil wells on their land. Brett now handled the wells, leaving the beef production to him and Reed, working with the livestock and the comradeship he enjoyed with the hired hands what he loved best about ranching.

Spending hours a day riding the range afforded him the chance to indulge in the solitude he still craved when the guilt returned without warning. If the haunting memories arose at night, blurring the line between his morals and the need to protect others, he would sit in the barn's open loft doors. He found peace in gazing at infinity through the star-studded inky sky.

Lately, though, it was the new neighbor who plagued his thoughts, which bugged him as much as his presence appeared to bug her. He had to admit, she'd done an admirable job covering her pique at their intrusion the other day. The only time he noticed it was when she looked at him, and damn if that annoyed spark in her blue eyes didn't make him itch to pin her against a wall and cover her mulish mouth with his. Given his sexual preference for control and her penchant to shun most people, including him, that would never happen, but it didn't prevent thoughts of her from distracting him.

She's an anomaly, that's all. Like every other challenge in life, he'll deal with it then move on.

Until then, Slade planned on staying clear, which was what he told Allie this morning when she tossed out Nicole had mentioned wanting a horse but lacked riding or equine care experience. There were other options around here where she could get both. He was too busy to add another chore to his schedule. A shout from one of the hands cut off the nagging voice calling that excuse an outright fabrication. This time of year, work slowed down from the busy spring and summer months.

A shrill whistle refocused his attention, and he nudged Bandit forward to meet up with Keith and Riley riding his way. He'd narrowed down his suspect list to one person responsible for the malicious, costly vandalism incidents around the ranch during the last fifteen months. For the life of him, though, he couldn't figure out why this part-time college student held a grudge against them.

"Hey, boss," Riley greeted him, the three of them reining to a stop a few feet from a red-coated, heavily pregnant cow. "We've pulled this one and two more to bring into the barn. A few others we're not sure about."

"Katy. She's so young." Keith pointed to one of the cream-coated Charbrays who grazed with a barely discernible baby bulge.

He shook his head at the kid. "I've warned you about naming them. It makes it that much harder on you come market time."

Keith eyed the young mother-to-be with fondness. "They don't *all* have to end up on someone's table, do they?"

Riley snorted. "They'd be out of business if they didn't. Right?"

Not quite, but he had a point. "We don't maintain a herd this size for pets." Slade remembered the calf his dad gave him to raise and still didn't believe their foreman's excuse she had been put down due to illness. "Now, what aren't you telling me? Where's Evan and Jeff?" All four were assigned to this herd today.

"You tell him," Keith insisted, his tone with his friend disgruntled.

"Hey, we tried talking them out of it." Facing Slade, Riley said, "They took off after an elk bull they saw in the woods."

Slade tensed with a grip of fury. There

was no time for them to dress a kill and haul it back and finish moving this herd, so what the hell were they thinking? Before he could tamp down his anger, the pair emerged from the trees, close enough he could see their grimaces when they spotted him. The only thing working in their favor was the absence of gunfire echoing through the woods, a sure sign the chase was unsuccessful.

He didn't waste time or words when they rode up. "You'll both be docked a half-day's wage. Get back to work."

Evan's usual resentful expression never changed, but Jeff's face reflected relief as he replied, "Thanks for not firing us, boss. Won't happen again."

This crap is going to end, he vowed, watching the four of them return to their positions around the herd. Slade didn't need one more thing tugging at his conscience and never took firing someone lightly. But damn it, his patience did have its limits.

Working with the guys, he helped drive the herd down to a lower pasture much closer to their barns where they would fare better come winter. Everyone's tension eased when Jeff and Keith started joking around as they kept the horde of cattle together and moving at a steady pace. After sending him a few guarded glances, even Evan cracked a few smiles before they rode into the stable yard. When he dropped the attitude, the kid revealed a passion for ranch work and demonstrated a genuine fondness for animals, especially his current mount, Tuck. He always chose the brown quarter horse from the corral if one of the other hands wasn't already riding him when Evan got here.

Slade dismounted at the rail, unsaddled Bandit, and turned him loose. He waited for the guys to release their horses along with the guys' mounts before crooking a finger at Evan. "A word, please."

Evan cast a look of unguarded longing toward the grazing horses before showing him his usual indifference. When the other three entered the stable, he asked, "Am I fired?" as if he didn't care one way or another.

Leaning against the corral posts, he crossed his arms. As with Nicole, there was something about the kid's attitude that reminded him of himself. "I should. You've been warned, repeatedly. Why?"

"Why what?"

"Why did you apply here, why do you stay if you dislike the job or me that much, or what's your grudge? Take your pick." He'd caught moments when Evan appeared to love ranch life, which didn't jive with his behavior.

Evan gave him a cocky grin. "Who wouldn't want a chance to work for the illustrious Kincaid brothers?"

Petty jealousy or something deeper he wasn't getting? "Not many would turn down the opportunity if ranching was what drew their interest. So, either you've discovered it's not your thing, or you applied for another reason." Oh yeah. That hit a nerve. That backbone went ramrod stiff, his hands curling into fists at his sides.

"Am I fired or not? I rode here with Riley."

"Not today," he returned, giving up for now. The kid presented a puzzle he was determined to solve. "But it is your last warning and final pass. See you Monday."

He nodded, a flash of relief in his green eyes before he turned and jogged to rejoin his friends. A definite conundrum Slade was determined to figure out. Driving home, he pondered what he could do about Evan short of letting him go or accusing him outright of the vandalism going on this past year. The answer still eluded him when he pulled up to his garage, but hearing Sam's excited barking as soon as he opened the door took his mind off Evan. The loud clatter of boards coming together filtered through the trees, and he wondered what his neighbor was up to now. She'd told them on Sunday the contractor wouldn't start until next week, so, unless she'd already hired other help, she was working on her own again.

Slade admired her drive, insisting he wasn't concerned about her doing any heavy lifting or using tools he doubted she was familiar with. She was a grown woman who obviously preferred solitude. And hard work to keep her mind off…something. He respected that, and, besides, whatever had brought her to Wyoming to live alone in such a remote area was none of his business. He should call Deb and go out to Casey's for a few hours. Spending time upstairs in their private space with his favorite play partner ought to relax him and take his mind off both Evan and Nicole. Deb loved bondage and leather, a multistrand flogger her favorite for him to apply.

For dinner, he tossed a couple of burgers on the grill, refusing to come up with something else just to avoid hearing any commotion from the other side of the woods. No one had done anything on Studman's property for over a year, not since Cecil had asked him to check on it once in a while before going into assisted living. When it sold at auction, he was glad someone would put the land to good use. He'd grown used to the quiet was all. Why else would he continue to get distracted and bothered by the slight noise coming from that direction?

Slade carried the done burgers inside, wondering if Nicole would take a break to eat then swore he didn't care one way or another. When he called Deb after downing dinner and couldn't come up with a valid reason for the relief he felt when she didn't answer, he gave up battling his curiosity. He changed into a heavier shirt to ward off the late-afternoon chill and traipsed through the woods again, telling himself this meant nothing more than doing the neighborly thing by checking up on someone.

Silence reigned around the yard as he strode toward the barn and stack of old lumber piled a few feet from the open door. He spotted nails sticking up on several worn slats before going inside. "Nicole, it's Slade," he called out, not seeing her or Sam. Taking a quick look around, he found the old stalls she'd started tearing down. Figuring she might have gone into the house to eat or quit for the day, he couldn't bring himself to walk away without finishing this task for her.

I'm saving her a little time and days of aching muscles. Slade swore that was the motive behind his help, which didn't explain the leap in his pulse when he emerged from the barn with an armful of boards and saw her stomping toward him with a scowl.

"Why are you here again?" she demanded, hands going to her slim hips.

His perverse side got a kick out of riling

her. Why, he couldn't answer yet. "I'm assisting you with this chore." He dropped his arms, and the wood fell on top of the pile. "That should be obvious."

Nicole turned her head, but he could still hear her mutter, "There's something seriously wrong with you."

"Why, because I'm friendly?"

"No, because I'm not. Hence, there's something wrong with you because you keep showing up anyway," she snapped, facing him again.

Well, that was honest and gave credence to the saying on today's shirt – *If you don't like my dog you probably won't like me – And I'm ok with that.*

Damn it, he really didn't want to like the woman. Before he could come up with a truthful reply, she bent to pet Sam who pressed against her leg at her angry voice. The over-large sweatshirt fell to the side on one shoulder, revealing a jagged scar that disappeared down into the sleeve. Slade's usual firm control slipped enough to propel him forward, force his hand to cup her upper arm, and bring her close enough for him to confirm the knife wound. Fury toward whoever had harmed her coiled in his abdomen like a rattlesnake preparing to strike.

"Hey, knock it off!" Nicole jerked her arm, and he released her, taking a deep breath to get himself under control. Yanking her sleeve back up, she shot daggers at him without backing away. "You need to leave."

Did that bravado stem from the attack or rile her assailant further? The strength of his anger on her behalf shocked him. Not that he was immune to the suffering of others, but he'd never reacted with such potent emotion with anyone except his family, especially without knowing the facts behind the injury. The thought of Nicole suffering such a painful, possibly dangerous ordeal produced a knot in his throat he couldn't swallow past.

"What happened?" he demanded. "I have firsthand experience with weapons, know what kind of damage a vast assortment of them can cause, what scars they can leave behind. That is a knife wound."

"Good for you, and none of your business. Go away."

Slade took a moment to study her face and body language, correlating her rigid stance and uneasy expression with how he had felt when someone would pry into the reason for his abrupt departure from the military. Like her, he hadn't wanted to talk about the incident that had such a profound effect on him with anyone, not even his brothers. He could now sympathize with how difficult it must have been for them to leave him alone when he insisted.

But Slade couldn't let it go until she answered one burning question. "Is he locked up?"

Nicole's eyes turned frosty. "No."

Not what he wanted to hear. "Why not?"

"Because I killed him."

*****

Nicole should to stop blurting it out like that. She'd shocked a few nosy people already with her blunt reply to questions about her attacker, receiving no satisfaction from their surprise. Slade's jolted reaction also conveyed relief, which, of course, rubbed her wrong.

"You preferred hearing a man is dead?"

"Don't put words in my mouth or attempt to read me, Nicole. We'll get along much better that way. It's getting dark and cold, but come help me and we can finish what you started in no time."

She had enough guilt plaguing her, so, instead of apologizing, she took him up on that offer without comment. They hauled out the last of the torn-down stalls in comfortable silence, finishing in no time with his help. Dusk had fallen along with the temperature when they emerged from the barn carrying the last few slats. With a shiver, Nicole unloaded hers onto the heap, glad the outside lights on the house and barn came on automatically.

"That will make a good bonfire," Slade commented, waving a hand toward the lumber pile, his tone much smoother compared to the deep rumble of his earlier hostility. "Not much else you can do with them since they're rotted through, and bonfires make a good excuse to get together with your friends."

"I don't know anyone here that well yet," she returned, his low voice in the semi-dark raising goose bumps. From the light above the barn door, she could see the lower half of his bristled face, but his hat shielded his eyes.

"You won't get to know anyone, staying out here. I'm surprised you're not uneasy living alone this far from town, unable to see another house." He turned his head, as if scanning the area around the house then stepped closer to Nicole, near enough for his body heat and large frame to warm her.

Nicole rubbed her arms, not about to tell him there were moments at night when either the silence or the strange animal sounds made her wish for company. During the day, when she was busy and the sunny blue sky revealed the beauty of her property, the solitude worked to soothe her unsettled emotions if she'd suffered through another night of guilt-ridden dreams.

"I'm from Chicago. Not much scares me, and I prefer the quiet. The city's never this peaceful. Shouldn't you call someone to give you a ride home?" she asked, noticing how much darker the woods were.

Slade reached out, catching her off guard as he clasped her hand with a tug toward the house and a chuckle that rumbled from his chest. "I already texted Reed, and I believe that's him coming up your drive. I noticed you didn't offer to run me back."

It took a moment for his last comment to register, her concentration blindsided by the tingles traveling from his warm, calloused grip up her arm. Disgusted with herself for allowing him to muddle her attention like a hormone-driven teenage girl, she yanked her hand out of his. "I'm not nice, remember?"

They reached her back door and stood under the light, Sam going around them to run inside as Slade opened the door, saying, "I'm not, either, but you remind me of myself about ten years ago. I would hate to see you, or anyone else, make the mistake I did by shutting out others. Call me or someone in the family if you hear or see something that leaves you unsettled. We'll check it out. And don't get cranky and delete my number after I leave." Reed honked, and Slade pressed a hand to her lower back, urging her inside as if she needed prodding to turn away from him. "Good night, Nicole."

"Thanks for the help," she managed to reply in a civil tone before closing the door and leaning her head against the hard wood. Nicole groaned, baffled and annoyed with the instant rise in her temperature from a simple touch. Slade had made no apologies or excuses when she had greeted his unexpected arrivals with coolness instead of gratitude, ignoring her unenthusiastic welcome to continue as he pleased. His family had been just as determined to assist her in any way, insisting on giving her their phone numbers after Slade jotted down his. Tony was the only stranger she'd met who turned out to be that genuine and nice. Regardless of their good intentions, she didn't want or need another man, or his family, on her doorstep every day.

Nicole had to eat those words the next morning when Lily called and asked if she wanted to meet Paul Westman, the man who had been floundering since losing his family. Lily's timing was perfect, catching her as soon as she crawled out of bed, groggy after a restless night imagining every creepy villain from the slasher movies she used to watch hiding out on her property.

Damn Slade Kincaid for putting that in her head.

She gave Sam ample opportunity to romp outside while she ate a quick breakfast and downed coffee before dressing. Those vivid dreams left her eager to hire someone willing to live in the cottage once Jim completed the few repairs and laid new flooring, the first chores she would ask of him come Monday. The long drive into Casper eased her tension from the sleepless night, Lily's early invitation giving Nicole time to shop a discount furniture outlet. Her mood improved tenfold after finding everything she needed to furnish the cozy space then locating the shelter using GPS and Lily's instructions.

Slade's soon-to-be sister-in-law was waiting for her outside, her long dark-brown hair pulled into a braid and wearing navy slacks paired with a cream, ribbed light sweater. Nicole slid out of her SUV, returning

Lily's wave as she closed the door. The clouds hid the sun's warmth, turning the air cooler than she'd felt since moving here.

"I'm so glad you could make it in today," Lily said, opening the door to a spacious entry. "The director called me when Paul showed up for breakfast, and she talked him into staying until I could take a lunch break. He's interested in the job, which pleases everyone who helps at the shelter and has gotten to know him. I can't imagine losing my family the way he did, then his job and home when he couldn't cope."

"No, I can't, either." Nicole never took for granted her parents' love and support, or the way her two closest friends had stood by her without question after Tony's death. "If he works out, this saves me a lot of time, and your recommendation eases my mind about asking him to live so close with no one else around."

"No worries there. Reed did an extensive search on Paul and found he has a clean record as far as any criminal activity. Not even a traffic ticket. This way."

She got a quick look at the main room

filled with tables that were over half full with a line at the buffet as Lily veered down a short hallway. The man waiting inside the office stood and faced them, clutching a worn baseball cap. With thinning gray hair and a lined face, he looked older than the forty-one Lily mentioned.

"Mr. Westman." Nicole held out her hand in the hope of putting him at ease. "I'm Nicole Wells. Thank you for talking to me today."

"Paul," he replied, taking her hand. His gaze slid toward Lily as she took the chair behind the desk.

They sat down, and Nicole explained the job, which involved preparing to take in rescued dogs and then assisting with their care, and the salary, which included the use of the cottage. "Are you okay with living in the country? Lily lives nearby if that helps."

"She mentioned that. I've always liked dogs. I used to have...a long time ago..."

Nicole gave his arm a brief touch, his genuine grief sealing her decision. "Recently, I suffered a great loss and understand the desire to escape from everything that reminded me of it. The cottage is small, but it will be furnished, the kitchen and bathroom stocked with necessities, and ready next week. Think about it, and let Lily know your decision."

Paul asked a few questions before standing again, still clutching the cap. "If you're willing to take a chance on me, I accept your generous offer."

Lily came around the desk, her face reflecting relief. "That's a good decision, Paul."

"For both of us," Nicole stated, hoping he wouldn't let depression or doubts alter his decision before he even started. He appeared grateful for the chance to work again, but an unexpected reminder of his loss could change his mind about reversing the course of his life. "I'll let Lily know when the cottage is ready." She waited until he left the office before turning to Lily. "Thanks for this. Fingers crossed it will benefit us both."

"If the director and I didn't think he was ready, we wouldn't have brought it up to him. Keeping him thinking positive will be the hard part. I don't have time for lunch, but Allie and I want to invite you to go with us to Casey's this weekend," she replied as they returned to the parking lot. "It's a club the guys own – music, dancing, a mechanical bull if you're daring enough."

"Ina mentioned it, and it would depend on how many drinks I have whether I can get up the nerve to get on that. Thanks. Can I let you know?" she asked, hesitating due to the likelihood of spending that time around Slade. Restricting her activities because of a man who got under her skin one second and roused her senses the next pissed her off enough to change her mind. "On second thought, yes, I'll go, but I'll meet you there. I may not stay as long as you." There. She felt better already.

"No problem. I'll send you directions and the time. Thanks again for taking a chance on Paul. He's a good guy and has helped a lot around the shelter."

Nicole knew only too well how difficult it could be coping with loss and still couldn't imagine the depth of his pain. She hoped the job would help him find the peace he needed to heal. A goal she herself could attain faster if her neighbor would quit intruding on her time and thoughts.

Chapter Six

Slade joined Jordon, their club manager, behind the bar, wishing Deb could have made it tonight. Now, he couldn't rely on her to keep his attention off Nicole. He picked up a whiskey glass from under the bar top, questioning whether his and Deb's long-term friends-with-benefits relationship would have been enough to keep him from thinking about those scars. Every time he imagined Nicole suffering such pain and fear, he went taut with fury. He was glad the bastard was dead but wished someone else had taken him out, suspecting the guilt weighed on her. Something he was all too familiar with.

"Are you going to pour that or stare at it all night?"

Jordon's amused tone broke into his thoughts and tore his gaze off the liquor bottle and glass he held. "I'm getting there," he muttered, the music and volume of the crowd filling Casey's tonight getting on his nerves.

"Couldn't talk one of your brothers into filling in for you tonight, huh?"

Slade moved down a few steps to hand the drink to the patient customer who nodded his thanks. "I didn't ask them," he said, turning toward Jordon.

He had agreed to go in on the club and put in the same amount of sweat equity as Reed and Brett to renovate the auctioned-off old lodge, knowing the social commitment required. They only opened Friday and Saturday nights, the three of them proud of the club's popularity and good reputation. When Lily mentioned inviting Nicole tonight, his first inclination had been to make an excuse to switch shifts with Reed, who planned to assist behind the bar tomorrow night. Instead, the constant urge to check on her all week, ensure she was okay, won out over his need to keep his distance.

"I intended to spend time upstairs with Deb later, but she made plans with her sister-in-law. Where's Bianca tonight?" Jordon and his longtime girlfriend had recently married, and with Brett and Reed settling down, that left scant few members of their private play group still single.

"Attending some kitchen gadget party, where she'll order stuff she'll never use." Nodding to the woman holding up her glass for a refill, he said, "Reed and Brett just came in. If you need to head home, feel free. I can always snag one of them if I get behind."

"Thanks, but I'm good." Besides his family, Jordon was the only other person aware of Slade's occasional moody silences and need for solitude when plagued by his war memories.

He glanced toward his brothers and couldn't prevent the quick jolt at seeing Nicole enter before the others reached the bar. She paused, scanning the filled tables separating the bar from the dance floor, her face as unsure as he was about her being here tonight. He'd tried telling her shunning others wouldn't help her burden, whatever it was, and admitted he was proud of the attempt she was making. That didn't mean he had to entertain her tonight though. There were plenty of other people around for her to hang with.

"You're here." Allie feigned surprise as she settled on a stool, the dangling row of small colorful balls hanging from her ears swinging against her chin. She smiled at Nicole's approach then said, "I half expected you to cancel."

He shrugged, refusing to let her obvious reference get to him. "I'm on the schedule."

Brett squeezed her nape with a warning to his wife. "Stay out of it, Allie."

Reed sat down and hauled Lily onto his lap and sent his brother an amused look. "Good luck with that."

Slade had to agree. Allie's manipulations put Reed and Lily together when neither suspected to see the other following a month-long separation. Instead of thinking about how well that had worked out for them, he asked, "Who wants what?" He started filling their drinks as Allie joined them, saved from greeting her when Lily pushed out a stool next to them.

"Here, sit between Allie and us. We're so

glad you came."

"Thanks. It's a popular place," she commented, avoiding glancing his way as she sat down.

"Location and luck, mostly. Have a drink on us as a welcome," Brett insisted.

Shifting a few steps her way, Slade couldn't keep from zeroing in on the edge of her scar peeking from the loose cowl neckline of her light-blue sweater or noticing how the color matched her eyes. Those eyes were pretty, the scar a reminder of the ugliness she'd endured, sparking a desire to replace the pain with pleasure. Imagining her reaction were he to suggest getting that close for an hour or two almost dared him to go for it.

"What can I get you?" he asked, the impact of the turmoil swirling in her direct, bright-blue gaze hitting his solar plexus as hard as a one-two punch.

"Bourbon and seven, light please. I'm driving."

Reed leaned around Lily to say, "Responsible. I like that. I'm glad you've hired someone and won't be out there alone much longer."

That news relieved Slade also. After learning of the attack on her, he couldn't deny how much her isolation bothered him. He set her drink down, compelled to add to his brother's comment. "Living outside the city comes with its own set of risks, one being the longer time it takes for help to arrive in an emergency. Having someone nearby is a good thing."

Nicole smiled, and some of the hesitancy with coming out tonight let up on her face. "Okay, I admit I've felt better since talking to Paul. Thanks again, Lily. I hope he's still looking forward to the move."

"He is." She rested a hand on Reed's forearm wrapped around her waist. "There's comfort in having a guy around a lot."

Allie chuckled. "Is that what you call it?"

"Excuse me," Nicole said abruptly. "Thanks for the drink. I'm going to check out the activity on that mechanical bull."

She walked away carrying her glass, but not before he caught a glimpse of sadness in her eyes. He might not like it, or want it, but his curiosity and the need to distract her from the memories of that painful incident weren't going away, only increasing.

Jordon's wife arrived, and he took a break to dance with her, leaving Slade busy behind the bar, but not enough over the next fifteen minutes to prevent him from keeping tabs on Nicole. She'd watched several people ride the gyrating vault designed to move similar to a bucking bull before someone asked her to dance. He knew a lot of their regulars, but not this guy, and didn't care for his taut reaction when the tall blond pulled her flush with his body. There was nothing untoward about the placement of his big hands on her lower back, except Slade discovered he wanted to be the one that close to her enticing butt showcased in those tight jeans.

"Hi there."

Shifting his attention away from Nicole, he ignored the brunette's flirtatious smile and asked, "What can I get you?"

"Screwdriver, please. You weren't here last time I was. Are you new?"

"Not hardly." He turned to retrieve a small orange juice from the under-counter refrigerator behind him and proceeded to mix her drink with his back to her. With luck, that would dissuade any more small talk. Instead, she jabbered away loud enough, her high-pitched voice carried over the music, grating on his nerves.

"Are you sure, 'cause I definitely would have noticed you. I just split with my boyfriend, the two-timing jerk. My friends all warned me about him, but I didn't listen. Live and learn, I guess. How about you?" she continued as he set her drink down. "Seeing anyone?"

"I see a lot of people." He tried but couldn't pull his hand away fast enough to avoid the caress of her fingers along his arm.

"How about a dance when you take a break?"

"How about you —"

"Kincaid, how the hell have you been?" Dave Marsh, a friend from high school, thrust a hand across the counter in greeting. "It's been a while."

"Too long," Slade agreed, mentally thanking him for his timely interruption. Too bad it didn't deter his customer.

"Kincaid? You're one of the brothers?" Her eyes gleamed with greedy lust, a reminder of Nicole's more appealing down-to-earth personality.

"The troublemaker when we were in our teens," Dave told her then addressed Slade again. "Listen, I gotta get back to our table after I get an order, but let's catch up soon."

"Definitely," Slade replied, now ignoring the woman altogether. From her frown, she wasn't happy. Tough. He was working and wasn't interested. No, his interest seemed to stay glued on Nicole, eyeing the sway of her hips as he mixed two drinks for Dave.

No sooner had Dave and the woman walked away than Brett strolled over and took their place with an amused glint in his eyes. "You once told me when you get an itch, you scratch it and it goes away."

"Your itch didn't," he taunted in return. That had been over a year ago, when Brett was fighting his attraction to Allie because of their age difference.

Cocking his head, Brett asked, "Is that what you're afraid of, if you act you'll get hooked?"

Ridiculous. Cutting his gaze toward Nicole again, he caught her quick grin as the couple separated and swore the spike in his pulse when she kissed the guy's cheek meant nothing. "Not in the least," he replied.

Brett chuckled. "I can warn you, lying to yourself won't help, but you won't listen. I'd say she's as closed-minded about a serious relationship as you, so neither one of you has anything to lose. No one is using the upper floor tonight. Just saying."

Slade glared at his brother's back, thinking he'd taken a page out of his wife's book for meddling. Nicole was snagged for another dance, and he experienced the same gut-clenching reaction. *Aw, what the hell,* he decided as Jordon returned.

"Your turn. Take your time. Things are slowing down."

"Thanks." Cursing Brett, Slade wound through the tables, bypassing attempts at conversation with a nod or wave on his way to scratch a fucking itch. The blood-pumping anticipation flowing through his veins didn't mean a damn thing, he swore, except a chance to appease his curiosity about her attacker and basic attraction.

***

There's comfort in having a guy around a lot.

Nicole regretted coming out tonight when Lily said that, those words describing her relationship with Tony and what she missed most. But comfortable friendship and profound caring didn't equate to love, and that guilt still lived inside her, day in and day out.

She sighed in relief when the slow ballad ended and she stepped back from her dance partner, more than ready to leave until she went hot upon seeing Slade. He was wearing his hat again, but she didn't need to see that pewter gaze clearly to feel the impact of his focused look or see the rigid set to his bristled jawline. Nicole didn't care for the man, and she sure as heck wasn't comfortable around him the way she'd been with Tony, but her neglected libido refused to listen to the rest of her.

Regardless, she wasn't in the mood to spar with him. After thanking the man for the dance, she headed toward the table where she'd set her glass down, the throng of people and loud music turning her hands clammy. Her breathing hitched, and she grew desperate for space and air, the sudden reaction coming out of nowhere. Veering toward the exit, luck eluded her as she bumped right into Slade's rock-hard body.

"Sorry," she muttered, attempting to go around him, needing the cooler, quieter outdoors.

"Come on." Taking her hand, he tugged her to the doors and outside, as if he'd read her mind.

Nicole filled her lungs, the cold compared to inside almost painful, her tension easing as the door closed behind them, muting the din. She'd gotten too used to going out with Tony to quiet bars or a movie, or just staying home, then isolating herself both at home and since moving here. It had been a mistake to ignore her instincts to pass on Lily's invitation.

"Crowds would do that to me when I first

returned home from the military. It'll pass. Until then, don't drive. We can..."

"Don't tell me what to do." Slade's deep voice erased the last dregs of her uncharacteristic panic, but it was the calming effect of his large, rough hand holding hers that she wasn't prepared for and didn't want to like. "Let go of me," she insisted when he tightened his fingers instead of releasing her when she pulled.

"Not until I'm sure you're okay."

Her fury was way out of proportion, given his concern, yet that didn't stop her from trying to take a swing at him. She gasped as he caught her uplifted arm by the wrist, spun her around, and pinned her against the building, away from the lighted doorway.

"Now, listen," she panted, head tilted as he towered over her, shielding her from anyone else's view with his wide shoulders.

"No, you listen." Slade lifted her shackled wrists and held them against the wood wall. "You need to let go of the anger or it'll eat you alive."

Nicole was too busy trying to tamp down the surge of heated lust inflaming her senses to fight his controlling move, but she managed to sneer, "Three uninvited visits, and you think you know me?"

"Getting there. I've told you I've been there. The difference is, I came home to friends and family who helped, whether I wanted them to or not. You ran away." He moved in closer, until their bodies touched, chest to pelvis, robbing her of breath and words as he whispered in her ear, "When the nightmares threatened my sanity, I found a friend who understood my needs and spent hours getting back in touch with my humanity."

Nicole's pulse spiked, and her breathing hitched as he raised his head. Her heated response to his dominant, caveman tactic shocked her, the lust coiling low in her abdomen hotter than anything she'd experienced before. "You're talking sex," she whispered.

"Am I?" He slid one hand behind her nape, his thumb resting against the pulse on the side of her neck. Sharp teeth sank into her lower lip, the sting ricocheting down to her toes, and she latched onto his forearm with her free hand to anchor against the onslaught of heightened sensation.

Damn. Tony had been nice, even in bed, the sex good but nothing that left her panting for the next round. Sex with Slade would be a lot like him, rough but focused on her, and she could go for that right now.

She licked her lip then brushed her mouth against his before returning the bite. "Sex I can do. Not interested in anything else."

"Then we're on the same page for once." Stepping back, he yanked her toward a side staircase she just now noticed, a small light turned on above the door at the top.

"Now?" she stuttered, following him up the stairs, her pussy going damp, her heart beating triple time. Shoving aside all hesitancy and *what-ifs* in favor of a temporary reprieve from grief and guilt wasn't easy until his calm matter-of-fact answer floated back to her.

"Why wait?"

She loved the way he simplified the matter and entered the darkened room without pause, confident enough people watched them leave the club together from downstairs to ease any worries. He surprised her, though, when he left the door ajar, enough for the overhead light to change the pitch-black to pearl gray along one side. She barely made out the stone fireplace and guessed that was a small bar in the far corner.

"What is this room?" she asked as he strode forward.

"A playroom."

Nicole's legs bumped into a sofa right before she found herself sprawled on her back on the wide leather seat, Slade's big body covering hers. She huffed a laugh – that alone felt good – and looped her arms around his neck. "Is the neighbor boy going to share his toys?"

"Not tonight," he returned, tugging her top up to slip his hand under. "Well, maybe one." He flexed his hips, grinding his thick cock against her mound as he covered her mouth.

A wave of potent need consumed her, and her humor fled, lust once again taking precedence. Nicole returned the kiss, her lips clinging to his then parting from the pressure.

Her low groan vibrated between them as their tongues danced, sending ripples of pleasure through her bloodstream. She tried arching against his groin, unable to budge because of his weight, and demonstrated her frustration by pinching his side. In retaliation, he shoved her bra up and delivered a much sharper squeeze to one unsuspecting nub, the snap of pain sending a lightning bolt of heat straight down to her pussy.

Slade lifted his head a fraction and spoke against her mouth, his lips brushing hers as he asked, "There's a bed down the hall. Continue this there, here, or do you want to call a halt?"

The matter-of-fact way he phrased that she took as a challenge, but, given her rapid, unexpected response to that small pain, Nicole wasn't about to back out now. "Here." She pushed her hands between them and sought his zipper. "Now."

Fumbling in the dark to get their jeans down took a lot of wriggling, shoving, and energy since Slade didn't seem inclined to take a minute to stand. That was fine by her. The faster, the better. She was already to the point of combustion and figured one quick round would last her a while at this rate. His heavy, hot flesh sprang into her hand, and she stroked up and down the thick length, brushing a thumb across the smooth damp crown, and savoring his indrawn breath until he pulled away.

"Enough." Slade punctuated the demand, spearing two fingers inside her, her body accepting the invasion with a damp surge. "You're tight. How long has it been?"

"None of your business," she replied smoothly, annoyed with the inquiry. Her long abstinence was why she wanted sex, not questions. "Do you want to do this or not?"

Instead of answering, he shoved his hand behind her neck, gripped her nape, and held her head still to grind his mouth on hers. She accepted the aggressive move with relief, his control freeing her of doubts and worries as he slowly withdrew his fingers, scraping her clit then tracing her bare labia while fumbling for a condom. Desperate for him to fill the emptiness inside her again, she snatched the latex from his hand and worked it over his thick, rigid length herself, clinging to his ravaging mouth.

His chest vibrated against hers with a low laugh as Slade lifted his head and released her nape. "Since you're in a hurry…" He bent her legs, kneeling on the sofa, leaving her jeans and panties at her ankles, then slid his hands under her cheeks to raise her pelvis. "Yes, I want to do this."

Nicole gripped his shoulders as he came forward, spreading her knees with his body to press his cockhead inside her. She almost wept from the pleasure/pain of his careful possession, aching for the mindless oblivion she craved from his body. Tony had given her slow and tender. Tonight, she needed just the opposite.

"I'm not fragile," she insisted, glad for the dark that hid the flush crawling up her neck and face from the thread of desperation in her voice.

"No, you're not. At least not at this moment."

With that cryptic remark hanging, Slade brought her pelvis up a notch and pushed harder, Nicole bracing for the reprieve she prayed this risk would give her.

*****

Nicole's face remained in shadows as Slade worked his way inside her snug pussy, making it difficult to read her. Her body quivered under his, her breathing rapid, which he'd put down to nerves if her tone hadn't conveyed such surety. He much preferred her lost in the throes of pleasure, though, instead of on the verge of a panic attack like downstairs. Recognizing the signs, he'd whisked her outside and taken control the best way he knew how, which was working damn well until he realized she'd abstained for a long period. He thrust harder, the grip of her slick muscles making it harder to stretch her tight walls, wishing he'd gotten her to open up about the attack before this. Knowing the facts would make it easier than second-guessing how far to push this tonight. He'd left the lights off on purpose so she couldn't make out the apparatus along the unlit side of the room. It wouldn't do to add to her stress by allowing her to walk in and see the bondage equipment and believe that's why he'd brought her here.

"Slade." Nicole dug her nails in hard enough he felt the prick under his shirt.

"More? You want more?"

"Yes," she insisted, her buttocks contracting in his hands with her attempt to move her hips.

He took her for her word, detecting no hesitation, and shifted his left hand from her ass to brace on his forearm by her head. Sliding his other thumb between her cheeks, he grazed her rear orifice and surged inside her pussy. She greeted his full possession with a soft cry and small contractions teasing his cock, her eager acceptance spurring him to pump faster, thrust harder. Nicole's orgasm burst swiftly, her sheath enveloping his straining cock, snug as a confining glove, and he grunted with effort to work through her spasms. The fire he'd ignited in her body was absolute torture, yet he basked in the flames snapping at sensitive nerve endings, driving him to the edge.

As his climax erupted with forceful jets of mind-fogging pleasure, Slade pressed his thumb harder against Nicole's tender anus than intended, slipping past the tight pucker. Her startled gasp ended with her teeth sinking into his neck, the sharp prick accompanying the delicate tremble of her muscles and one more small damp, quivering release. Her responsiveness drove home a point he couldn't deny or walk away from – once wouldn't be enough for either of them.

"Are you with me?" he asked, pulling out of her and running his hands up and down her smooth thighs.

"I'm here, yes," she returned, her voice steady.

"Good." Getting to his feet, he yanked his jeans up then bent to lift her over his shoulder, swatting her upturned butt as he strode toward the hallway. "We're going to get more comfortable for round two."

Chapter Seven

One minute, Nicole's attention was centered on the burning spot from Slade's butt whack, and the next on the soft mattress under her and his hands divesting her of her clothes. As eager as he to indulge in another go-around, she helped by toeing off her shoes and kicking her jeans off her feet. They stripped each other of their shirts, the tickle of his chest hair as he lowered himself, urging her to latch on for another wild ride. Panting, she searched for his mouth in the dark, chuckled at his low curses as she palmed his taut buttocks, and bowed her back with a gasp when he bit into a nipple. Instead of turning down the heat, the slight sting had the opposite effect, taking her from hot to feverish. She would analyze the oddity of that later, she decided when he grabbed her arms and lifted them above her with one of his unexplained commands.

"Hold on and don't let go."

"Why?" she muttered, wrapping her fingers around what felt like brass posts on a headboard.

Instead of answering, Slade ran his hands down her body, rotating his palms over her nipples before gliding down her sides and legs, his broad shoulders parting her bent knees wider. A low moan escaped with the scrape of his bristled jaw along the tender skin of her inner thigh. Nicole loved the dark that offered her the freedom to relish this temporary escape from reality. If it weren't for his bossiness and deep, distinctive voice, she could pretend she was with someone else, even if she couldn't deny the rough-around-the-edges cowboy did it for her at this moment.

Slade dug his fingers into the fleshy side of her hips and took a slow lick between her pussy lips, the soft touch igniting another firestorm of pleasure. She cried out as he tugged on her clit and sucked hard on the tender nub, her sheath spasming around the finger he added. Breathing heavy from her unexpected, rapid response, Nicole dropped her arms to grip his shoulders, needing the anchorage against the rising tide of hot, convulsive pleasure. The bulging muscles under his smooth skin were hard to hold onto, even more so when he pulled his mouth off her needy flesh way too soon.

Before she could complain, he pinched her leg, stating calmly, "Put your hands back."

"You just don't quit, do you?"

"Do you want me to?"

He would have to wait until she was ready to beg to ask that. "Damn, you're annoying. No, I don't want you to."

She wouldn't put it past him to be able to see in the dark if she tried to fool him and grabbed hold of the bars again. Her second orgasm of the night made the concession well worth putting herself in his hands for a few minutes. Those minutes stretched into at least thirty as he didn't bother pausing after she splintered apart under his mouth to surge over her and inside her again. Nicole strained against his heaving body, glorying in the extended oblivion and record-breaking third climax that drained her of energy but left her sated beyond measure.

Laughter and car doors shutting roused her a short time later, and Nicole jerked upright, the hallway light now shining into the room, revealing she was alone. The furnishings were scant, just the bed, an oversized stuffed chair, and an end table holding a lamp. Figuring Slade might be in the restroom, she chose the coward's way out and dressed in a hurry despite the tremors still coursing through her body and weak limbs. She heard water running behind the closed restroom door as she rushed by, but the odd contraptions along the wall in the main room halted her headlong dash to make a hasty exit.

Unable to resist, Nicole walked closer, her heart beating double-time imagining Slade tormenting someone he'd bound on a padded bench or secured on the dangling chains. She'd never harbored much curiosity about what went on in Chicago's kink clubs, not even after meeting someone in college who was a member. Now she couldn't keep from picturing herself lying naked on the bench in front of her, gazing up at Slade's sun-kissed face, ready and willing for him to do anything he desired as long as it led to the sweet oblivion she'd experienced earlier.

"If you're shocked, it's your own fault."

She snatched her hand off the bench, refusing to blush as she turned to see him striding toward her shirtless and barefoot, the awesome eagle tattoo spread over one shoulder and upper arm drawing her eyes. *That is so...sexy.* In the dark, she hadn't been able to make out much more than his large shape above her, feel anything except his flexing muscles as he drove into her, and heard nothing except his heavy grunts in her ear. Her vaginal muscles clenched to block the ache for another tangle in the sheets worming its way through her body, and she fought to stay put.

He halted close enough her nose almost touched his chest, and Nicole gripped her purse strap tighter, managing to resist the temptation to bridge that small gap. Proud of herself, she forced a smile. "Not shocked, curious. You've demonstrated your penchant for control tonight.”

“And you liked it.”

That blunt assertion nudged her a step away, reinforcing her backbone and determination not to get involved again. “The sex was good,” she returned without inflexion.

“Good enough to appease your curiosity?” Slade shifted his gaze from her to the bench.

Tempted by the offer, Nicole thought of the painful memories waiting to pounce when she went to bed and closed her eyes. But that would only provide another temporary reprieve. She needed more time and space, now that he’d appeased her lust.

“I have to get home to Sam.”

“How long ago?” he asked as she pivoted.

Puzzled, she faced him again at the same time he reached for her, his hands landing on her waist to draw her flush with his warm body. She steeled herself against the quivering tickle in her abdomen and latched onto those ripped arms. *Chemistry, that’s all.* She would work on believing that tomorrow.

“How long ago what?”

"Did you start thinking you're better off keeping to yourself after killing the person who attacked you."

God, she hated his astuteness. Steeling herself to resist this unwanted attraction, she pulled away from the loose embrace and griped, "Are you a shrink?"

"Hell no."

Slade huffed, fisting his hands on his hips, and she felt better. "Some weird guru?"

"No." Shaking his head, he stated, "Just someone who's been there. Killing someone even in self-defense isn't easy to live with."

"No, it isn't." Those gunmetal eyes were difficult to look away from, especially when they darkened with an emotion only he could label, tempting her to ask about his experience. Instead, since he gave a little, she did also. It wasn't like the incident was a big secret. "Six months, almost seven, but before you ask anything else, I really want to get home to Sam. He's not used to being left alone so long, and he's still adjusting to the new place." She could tell he was frustrated and champing at the bit for more, yet, for some reason, his nosiness didn't bother her as it should. Maybe she was getting used to his constant interference.

"Okay. Wait for me to finish dressing. I mean it."

And maybe not.

Before she could snap at the order, he rephrased the comment. "Would you wait for me, please?"

"Good catch," she couldn't resist replying with a quick grin. "Sure. Thanks for asking."

Shaking his head, as if bemused either by her or himself, Slade pivoted and strode down the hall. Nicole eyed the other half of the tattooed eagle's wings draped over his shoulder, the gray, black, and white feathers fanned open to cover his entire shoulder blade. She stood there mystified, unsure whether she found the man bothersome because of her desire to remain detached for a while or because of her heated response to everything physical about him, like that emblem.

She couldn't talk him out of following her home, although she didn't try too hard. There was some comfort to his presence, similar to what she experienced when with

Tony, yet the continuous frissons of fervid intensity that took over her common sense whenever she got close to Slade kept her on edge. Insisting she wasn't ready for anything hadn't stopped her from caving to lust. Hoping that was all her moment of weakness was, she reached the front door first and opened it to let Sam outside. Of course, the traitor dashed straight for Slade as he got out of the truck. Nicole flipped on another light, brightening the whole living space while keeping her hand on the door.

"All safe and sound," she told him the same time her phone jangled. Nicole fumbled in her purse to check the text, worrying since her parents were the only people who would try to contact her this late. Instead of seeing their name in the lighted display, it read *Anonymous* with the first part of the text, *You can run, but you can't*, showing underneath. It didn't take a brain surgeon to figure out the rest of the message, or who sent it. Swearing at Natalie's persistence, she hit delete and dropped it back inside her purse before she realized Slade could read that also.

"Problem, Nicole?" he asked, moving

closer. Needing him gone before she gave in to the weakness he'd tapped into earlier, she stepped back and shook her head, keeping hold of the door handle. "No. A spam text instead of who I thought it might be. Thanks for seeing me home."

"I get it. You want me gone." With one finger, he traced the scar on her neck, down her shoulder, the light touch searing her skin. "Take care, neighbor."

She didn't reply and watched him leave, the silence close to deafening once his truck turned onto the highway.

Despite the late night, Nicole awoke early to Sam's whine and cold nose nudging her arm. "Yeah, I know, you want out." She petted him and he pranced away with another whine, his tail whipping back and forth. Recognizing the signs, she rolled out of the warm bed and pulled on jeans and the sweatshirt lying at the foot, one of only a few gifts from Tony that she'd kept because he'd imprinted Sam's photo on the front. "Come on, then. God forbid you let me sleep in."

Maybe this was good practice for when

she had kids, she mused, opening the back door for Sam. Her heart ached at that thought, believing Tony would have been a good dad before the brain tumor. A sad reminder of how fast life can throw you a curve ball that changed everything.

Speak of altering curve balls, she mused, wincing as she sat down with a cup of coffee. The discomfort conjured up the other person she was trying hard not to think about. She'd never imagined ending over a year of abstinence would result in this soreness. Sex had always been a take-it-or-leave-it indulgence for her, happy to hit the sheets when in a relationship, but otherwise she had no problem living celibate.

Not until last night.

Damn, there went her promise not to dwell on Slade all day after spending a sleepless night dreaming about his every touch and the orgasms that had soared higher than anything she'd achieved before. With Tony, climaxes had flowed through her body, the sensation similar to standing in a slow-rolling warm tide. Slade's focused, driven thrusts sent her careening into a maelstrom of sensation overload that still lingered this morning.

Nicole couldn't quit thinking about him before his erotic hold on her wrists and deep, powerful thrusts drove her to such extreme, euphoric heights, which baffled her considering how much he annoyed her. Now, how was she supposed to forget all about him the same as she'd done every other man except Tony who had come and gone in her life?

Sam's excited barking pulled Nicole's head out of the clouds, and she dashed outside to check on him. "Sam, come!" she called out as soon as she spotted him running after a stray tan dog. He halted before following the other dog into the woods, thank goodness. She didn't relish going after him in the thick trees at the break of dawn. Even though he loved romping with other dogs, strays were unpredictable, and she would have to evaluate the ones in the shelter before socializing them with playtime. With luck, she could gain the other dog's trust, put some weight on him, then find him a home.

"Good boy." Nicole hugged Sam and

took him inside as her cell beeped with an incoming text. She stiffened, just now recalling last night's message. That was the third time Tony's sister had gotten hold of her new cell number, and if Natalie started constantly harassing her here as she did in Chicago, she would have no choice but to report the anonymous message even without solid proof it had come from Tony's twin.

She fed Sam first then glanced at the message, relieved when she read Allie's name and the intro line asking what happened to her last night. With a sigh of guilt, Nicole realized she'd taken off without telling either Allie or Lily, the two who had invited her in the first place. Slade must not have said anything, at least, not yet, and she couldn't help feeling grateful for his silence. The last thing she wanted was his family speculating on a budding relationship between them.

She texted, *Sorry. I was tired and left without thinking,* keeping it simple and truthful, and then vowed not to give either Slade or Natalie another thought. She had too much to do before the contractors arrived tomorrow to waste another moment on either one.

*****

Slade made it close to twenty-four hours before caving to the urge to check on Nicole. He blamed the constant yipping of more than one dog filtering through the woods, exciting Chase and interrupting his relaxation as he grabbed the take-out order from the diner and headed over at twilight. If she didn't welcome another uninvited visit, that was too damn bad. He had spent the day worried she would regret her actions last night and itching to inquire about that text. It could have been anything between an innocuous joke and a serious threat. Her hired help wouldn't start for a week, leaving her alone way too long for his peace of mind if it was the latter.

In a matter of two short weeks, his curiosity about the new neighbor had expanded into constant preoccupation that sex hadn't appeased. He wasn't sure what to do about that or her, so he went with his instinct that all was not right. When she convinced him otherwise, maybe he could get back to his original plan of friendly neighbor.

The hunger-stirring aroma of Ina's stroganoff tickled his senses, and his stomach growled in response, Chase following him to the door with his nose on the bag. When he put on his dejected face after Slade instructed him to stay, he figured his dog could join in on the fun too. If her shelter took on several dogs at once, Sam would benefit from early practice in getting along with more than the one.

"Come on, then. Let's see what kind of mood our neighbor is in today."

He tried not to think about the feel of Nicole's soft body moving under his, her gasps when she climaxed, or the effort it took to loosen her tight muscles. She hadn't resisted his hold, which surprised him, given her fierce independent streak, but he'd expected her withdrawal afterward. Getting her to open up about her ordeal might require him to do the same, something he was prepared to do if it would help.

Slade emerged from the forest trail to

witness Nicole trying to lure a coyote closer with dog treats. "Shit. Chase, go!" Border collies ran like the wind, and Chase had plenty of practice running off undesirable critters. Coyotes were timid animals around people and one on one with an aggressive dog, but a small pack could take down a horse or steer. This one bolted into the woods, leaving poor Sam looking bewildered and Nicole glaring at him. Obviously, she knew little about Wyoming wildlife.

Chase got a friendlier greeting from Sam than Slade did from Nicole as she stomped to meet him halfway. "Why the hell did you do that? You just ruined three days of trying to gain that dog's trust."

"Then you wasted your time on a coyote, not a dog. It could have been a hybrid, but either way, he was a wild animal that could have gone for Sam's throat two seconds after playing. You're welcome."

Nicole's hand went to her chest, her face paling. "I didn't know." She stepped back and stated stiffly, "Thanks."

He sucked in a breath, vacillating between annoyance and amusement. Those seem to be his two reactions around her if he ignored lust. Seeking some middle ground, he asked, "Ever heard of compromise?"

"Heard of it; don't much care for it."

"You and me both, but growing up with two brothers, I learned how to get along." He held up the dinner bag. "You lighten up, and I'll share Ina's beef stroganoff with you. Deal?"

Nicole's eyes sparkled as she tucked her short hair behind her ear where it curved under her chin, and then bent her head toward the bag and took a whiff. Whether she acknowledged it or not, the fact she exposed her scar without a thought proved she was already comfortable with him.

"Okay, deal. But only because I haven't eaten yet, and finding out how dumb I am about wildlife hasn't gone down well."

"Not dumb," he insisted, clasping her hand just to watch her frown as they walked to the house. "A lot of visitors and new residents make the same mistake. I would advise you take smaller rescues to the shelter in Casper. They are easy prey for not only the coyotes but hawks and owls."

"There's a lot I didn't consider when I settled on this endeavor." She opened the back door then cast a worried glance toward the dogs, who were running and tussling.

"They'll be fine. Chase will alert me if there's a threat." Dropping her hand, he held the door then followed her inside before propping the screen door open. "Feel better?"

She nodded and led the way into the kitchen where she got out paper plates and forks. If she was uncomfortable being alone with him again after last night, it didn't show when they sat down and dove into the creamy pasta. However, she was almost as good as he at hiding emotions.

"Oh, this is good." Looking up from her plate, she smiled. "Thanks, again."

A sucker punch of lust hit him so hard, Slade tightened his fingers on the fork to keep from reaching across the table to haul her on top of it. "No problem. I presumed you were outside with Sam when I heard him, and you hadn't eaten yet. I wanted to check on you, make sure you were okay, that I wasn't too rough."

Nicole scooped up another forkful of

stroganoff and ate it before answering. As far as he could tell, his blunt speaking didn't faze her. She swallowed and waved the fork, replying, "If you knew me better, you wouldn't have gone to the trouble. As you can see, I'm fine."

A bit put out by her blasé attitude toward an encounter that had plagued him for the better part of the day, he returned, "I can't read your mind, however, I understand you better than you think."

"No you don't."

It was the lack of hesitation in those three words that got to him. He kept eating while he spoke and proved it. "You left Chicago to run away from memories. You killed someone, presumably the person who attacked you, and the guilt is weighing on you. You've cut yourself off from family and friends, stayed out here where you're not answerable to anyone, and only want to care about your dog. Then reality slipped past your walls, and you needed supplies and help, which meant getting involved with people again. And, damn, people around here are so nice, thoughtful, and supportive, you can't say no. Now, you're running scared, not of the trauma or the perpetrator but of returning to living."

Nicole remained silent when Slade finished, her focus on her plate until she swallowed the last bite. Without commenting on his observations, she picked up their empty plates and carried them to the trash under the sink, talking over her shoulder. "I'll be sure and tell Ina how much I enjoyed that. From now on, though, please call me before stopping by. I'm going to be busy with the contractors starting Monday, so if you were hoping for a repeat of last night in appreciation, that's not going to happen."

Slade rose, refusing to rise to that bait as he picked up his Stetson off the chair to put back on. He couldn't fault her rigid refusal to give an inch because he'd acted the same for a long time, and six months wasn't long enough for those memories to fade. Nevertheless, he wouldn't walk away without responding to that taunt. "I expect you to face me when you're going to accuse me of something. I've been up front with you from when we first met. Don't ever assume otherwise."

Nicole's stiff shoulders sagged, and he let it go, unable to leave without offering a sounding board when she was ready.

"I've taken several lives, all in the act of saving others. You killed to save yourself. It helped to tell myself they were bad people with malicious intentions until my last assignment. When, or if you want to talk, you're welcome to drop in anytime. Follow the trail over the creek bridge until you see a house."

*****

Nicole waited until she heard Slade whistle for Chase, and Sam came barreling inside alone before turning from the sink to face the now-empty kitchen. The space had seemed much smaller and cramped with his large presence, and she breathed easier now that he'd left. She didn't care for the sudden flush of pleasure she'd experienced when she first saw him outside, or the gratitude she owed him for rescuing her from her folly about the mistaken coyote. It didn't bear thinking about what might have happened if he hadn't come over a few minutes after the animal returned. Worse, though, was the guilt from allowing him to think she believed he'd come here wanting sex again. She bemoaned letting the flood of emotions he opened get the best of her.

Sam practically plowed into her, and she bent to rub his chest, Slade's accurate assessment of her mental struggles still on her mind. Wasn't it bad enough she'd had to sit through dinner aching to repeat the mistake of sleeping with him? Sexual attraction had always been easy to define and either ignore or go for until he'd demonstrated the benefits of giving up control. The hours of letting go had freed her of guilt for a short time, a much-needed respite from regrets and loneliness, expecting it to end there. Instead, the second she heard his voice, she'd gone hot and damp, her quick response as annoying as his interference until he'd set her straight on the coyote. Her irritation turned inward after hearing she'd unintentionally put Sam in jeopardy.

"Tell me something, boy. How can I

want the man when I don't like him?"

Sam barked and wagged his tail, looking from her to the treat cabinet." You have a one-track mind, my friend, and are of no help to me in my hour of need."

Padding into the living room, she turned on the television, hoping to find something that would take her mind off Slade's last words. He'd said enough to figure he had been overseas in the military, seen and done things necessary to save lives, and that the last mission had not gone well, changing his perspective. Damn it, just enough to keep her curious.

Nicole threw herself onto the couch with a sigh. She didn't want to appreciate anything about the guy, or feel bad over the blunder he'd rightfully called her on. The possibility they might share something in common went down as well as owing him an apology. And she sure as heck was not happy to admit, one touch and she would strip naked, praying for him to jump her bones again. For the first time since leaving Chicago, she wished her mother or friends were here. After Tony's death, they became her rock and sounding boards, their honest feedback as truthful and welcome as his used to be since they knew her best.

Sam hopped onto the couch and laid his head in her lap, and she felt her melancholy slip away stroking his soft fur. Comparing the relaxed, happy dog snuggling next to her to the timid, scared pup that first arrived at the shelter reminded Nicole of the months of hard work and socializing it took to rehabilitate him. *Maybe I should apply that technique to myself,* she contemplated. She would see how the upcoming week went with people around all day and go from there. For certain, the way she'd been going about getting over Tony's death wasn't working.

Chapter Eight

After spending half the night pissed off at Nicole and the other half worried about her, Slade entered the stables the following morning itching for a battle. He spotted Evan nailing a new horseshoe onto Apollo's hoof with Reed's guidance. Instead of obliging his mood, Evan tossed a rare grin over his shoulder as he straightened, dropping the stallion's leg.

"Check this out. Not bad if I say so myself," he boasted.

Slade checked the hoof then looked at Evan, pleased with his improved disposition today. "Good job. Are you two done in here?" he asked Reed.

"We're done. Go ahead and join the others, Evan."

He waited until Evan was out of earshot

before saying, "Came in early and without attitude. I wonder why?"

"I'd rather enjoy the reprieve than waste time questioning it," Reed stated, stroking Apollo's brown-spotted neck. "Besides, you walked in with enough attitude for both of you."

"I was in battle mode, expecting another confrontation." He strode to Bandit's stall, and they led their mounts outside before Reed picked up the conversation.

"Is he the one responsible for the trouble lately?"

"Maybe. Likely."

They grabbed saddles and prepped the horses, the task not enough to keep his brother from digging for more. "You have proof or just suspicions?"

Slade mounted, not ready to discuss his hunch. "Nothing concrete. Where are we headed?"

"Hunting. We lost two calves last night. The tracks looked like cougar."

"Fucking cats." Pumas topped the list as one of the most elusive animals in the wild, making them difficult to track. They were also deadly when on the prowl and he left Chase behind. Better safe than sorry. He checked the ammunition in his rifle before riding out, saying, "Let's go hunting."

They rode at a brisk pace for thirty minutes, talking with gestures, before slowing enough to hear each other. He almost picked up speed again when Reed spoke without lifting his head from the recent tracks they found.

"So, what happened between you and our new neighbor last weekend at Casey's?"

"We spoke, and I followed her home." Slade pointed to a clear paw print in a muddy patch. "He's a big son of a bitch."

"And wily. The tracks disappear here."

They'd come upon a rocky foothill with no discernible pathways, easy enough for a mountain lion or skilled climber, which they weren't, to scale. Tugging on the reins, he steered Bandit to the right. "Let's circle a bit before giving up."

Reed kept his focus either downward, his lips curving as he said, "Sounds good. Gives you time to tell me how Nicole responded when you took her upstairs."

Slade wasn't amused but used to his brother's good-natured ribbing. "How did Lily respond in bed last night? Or did you take her upstairs?"

"Okay, I get it," he replied, glancing his way with a chuckle. "Gotta admit, though, I'm liking the merry chase she's leading you on."

The cat's loud snarl had them quickly withdrawing their rifles from the scabbards, seconds before they caught sight of a puma's tail. They followed with caution, luck staying with them when they saw the cat halfway up the hillside. In sync, they took aim and fired, dropping him a few feet away.

"He's even bigger than I imagined." Slade nudged the fallen puma with his rifle, making sure he was dead. He could see how easily an animal this size could kill a couple of calves in one attack.

"Damn, I wouldn't want this guy anywhere near our houses. There are stories of cats wandering into towns lately. Too bad we couldn't risk the time to contact one of the sanctuaries to take him though."

He shuddered, Reed's comment bringing

Nicole living alone with a timid dog to mind. "Let's get back."

The hunt took the better part of the morning, and he worked alongside Reed when they returned, playing catch-up on their chores. He couldn't seem to stop thinking about Nicole, worrying when there was no cause. She was a grown, independent woman, brave enough to tackle that run-down place on her own, so his fixation made no sense. He liked her spirit, admired her gumption, and couldn't deny his sexual attraction. There were other women he liked, a few he admired, and if he'd acted on every woman he found sexually attractive, his lifestyle would be no better than his philandering father's. Which left him asking where, or to whom, he went from here.

*****

He rubbed the saddle soap harder into the supple leather seat, unable to recall anyone else who had drawn all three responses, not even his long-time friend and part-time play partner, Deb. Maybe he should give her a call, ask if she cared to meet him at Casey's tonight. It had been a while since they had hooked up, and hanging out with someone he cared a great deal for might be what he needed to squash his increasing preoccupation with Nicole.

"What has your head in the clouds?"

Slade swung around to face Brett, Reed gazing at him with an amused expression that rubbed him wrong. "Nothing wrong with concentrating on work, is there? I didn't hear you. Sue me."

Brett nudged his hat up and cocked his head. "I thought it might be the neighbor again."

Scooping a hand through his hair to get it off his face, he asked, "Why would you think that?"

"Allie invited her to have coffee this morning." He looked over at Reed, saying, "Apparently, Nicole has Slade to thank for setting her straight on the difference between a stray dog and a coyote."

"She didn't." Reed sounded both surprised and worried as he asked Slade,

"She tried to get friendly with one?"

"With a dog treat," he drawled, pleased to hear Nicole was getting out instead of staying isolated.

Brett shook his head with a grin. "Okay, now it sounds amusing. Still, Allie thought someone should suggest she think about fostering the overload from Casper's shelter instead of tackling strays, at least for now."

Definitely time to give Deb a call, Slade decided when his pulse jumped at using that excuse to see her again. He turned back to his chore before asking, "Why didn't she suggest it?"

"Said she didn't want to come across as doubting her ability to handle the endeavor, whereas, that wouldn't bother you."

Reed's sawhorse holding his saddle stood close enough to Slade's for him to nudge him. "She's got a point."

"She's interfering again." He glared at Brett over his shoulder. "Tell her to knock it off and mention that to Nicole herself. Now, quit bugging me. Both of you."

The first thing Slade did when he arrived home was call Deb.

*****

"I've got to run. Ten o'clock meeting with a new client," Lily said, picking up her coffee cup.

"And I have errands to run." Nicole finished off her coffee then told Allie, "Thanks for having me over this morning, and for your suggestion to foster. You gave me something to think about. Your home is beautiful. "

She enjoyed the coffee, blueberry bagel, and small talk with sunlight pouring through the far wall of windows, spanning the den, dining, and kitchen area. Both Allie's invitation to join them for coffee and the idea about fostering had come at an opportune time. For the fifth morning straight, she'd awoken thinking about Slade. If that weren't annoying enough, instead of the sex scratching her itch, it seemed to have intensified with each passing day. On top of that, she owed him an apology, and she always paid her debts.

"Thank you. I love it out here." Allie

walked with them out to the front porch. "You're not upset that Slade mentioned the coyote incident, are you? According to Brett, he was worried. Not that he'd admit, of course."

Lily chuckled. "Not Slade. His protective streak is as strong as Reed's though."

"I'm glad I'm not the only one suffering his interference, even if I do appreciate his timely arrival the other evening. And no, it doesn't bother me that he told his brothers. It's nice they're close." Probably as close as she'd been to Tony, a bond she envied, and missed. While she didn't need anyone worrying about her, his concern had seeped through her armor and touched a soft spot she'd spent the week trying to harden again.

"Yeah, they are," Allie agreed, following them down the steps to the long drive and their vehicles. "But, according to Brett, it still took a few years to get him to open up about his job as a military sniper."

Lily opened her door and pointed to the east. "Our place is a mile in that direction, Slade's another mile beyond that."

With Lily right behind her, Nicole drove

down the long road to the highway, glancing across the rangeland the Kincaids owned, unable to resist searching for Slade among the handful of riders. The ranch buildings were far enough away she could barely glimpse the roofs, the same with the hands on horseback, and she turned onto the highway cursing her weakness. *What red-blooded, sane woman wouldn't lust after any of the Kincaid brothers?* That argument would work if Slade weren't the only brother who turned her into an inferno with one look, or a simple touch. As if that weren't enough, now she found herself sympathizing with the painful toll his years as a sniper must have taken on him.

Allie had mentioned joining them at Casey's again tonight, and her first inclination had been to decline, but she'd never let a man dictate her life and wouldn't start now. Besides, she was determined to go and *not* behave like a weak-kneed ninny when she apologized. Once she got that out of the way, maybe she would stop thinking so much about him.

The daily list of to-do tasks started with

laundry. With only one small load, she hoped to finish shopping in the mercantile, grab a sandwich, and return home with plenty of daylight left to hang outside with Sam and scratch a few more chores off her list.

Right on schedule, Nicole entered Ina's less than an hour later and took a seat at the counter, choosing the grilled chicken melt as Ina strolled over.

"Nice to see you again, Nicole. How's that shelter coming along?"

Pleased she remembered her, Nicole replied, "Barn and cottage are cleared, ready for the contractors on Monday." Which gave her only two days to plan on operating a shelter or accommodate numerous foster dogs.

"You've hired Baker Construction, I hear. Jim will do right by you. Dated his older brother a time or two. Before Howard, of course. What can I get you?"

Nicole ordered the sandwich special, bemused by Ina's rapid-fire dialog and subject changes. Her parents were lucky enough to enjoy a long, loving marriage, like the Hendersons, their relationship also going back to high school. None of her teen dates had made a lasting impression, let alone a desire for commitment. A much bigger school in a large city filled with people and opportunities might account for that, but already, she could tell the merits of growing up here.

"Thank you," she said when Ina came in with her order. Looking at the loaded plate, she groaned. "You didn't tell me it came with fries and a salad, or that you put a whole chicken in the sandwich."

"Just half a chicken, dear." She patted her hand. "I'll bring you a take-home box before you finish."

Nicole stepped out of the diner feeling full but good, happy with the day so far. With leftovers for dinner, she wouldn't have to cook, saving time before she left for Casey's. She would apologize to Slade, be done with that chore, and then have fun. Maybe get up the nerve to try the mechanical bull after a drink or two, she mused, and dance with a hot cowboy. Someone other than the hot neighbor.

She stepped off the sidewalk to cross over

to the cars, thinking about what she would say to Slade tonight, when a car came screeching out of a lane with the motor gunning. With only seconds to spare, someone acted faster than she could and grabbed her arm, yanking her out of harm's way to land with a jarring thud on the concrete as the car sped away too fast to identify the driver.

Shaken, her heart slamming in her chest, she lay there a minute, struggling to breathe until her savior lifted off her. Shoppers converged on them, everyone talking at once, asking if she was all right, what happened, did anyone catch who that idiot driver was.

"Did I hurt you? I'm sorry, I just reacted."

The older gentleman helped her stand, his concerned face swimming before Nicole's watery eyes as she worked to get herself under control. "I'm okay." She gave a weak laugh. "At least, I think so." Her thigh ached, but so far, that was the only repercussion she could detect.

Ina and another woman were suddenly there, the one she didn't recognize looking from her to the man. "Oh, my goodness! William, is she all right? These darn reckless teenagers!"

Ina interrupted, clapped her hands, and shooed everyone out of the way. "All taken care of. Let the poor girl catch her breath, everyone."

"Thanks," she told the three of them when the crowd dispersed. "My fault. I wasn't paying attention." She held her hand out to the man. "William? Nicole Wells, and I appreciate your quick thinking. I owe you one."

"Nonsense. I'm Andrea Hastings, and we're just glad you weren't hurt."

William smiled. "What my wife said."

Ina put an arm around her shoulders as they moved to the sidewalk. "Why don't you let one of us drive you home, dear?"

Damn it. Nicole's throat clogged, the small hug eliciting a longing for her mom. "I must be good. Look." She cleared her throat, held up the leftovers still in the bag, and quipped, "I managed to save the food."

William, bless him, took over for Nicole. "All right. Let the girl be on her way. Come along, you two."

Nicole thanked them again and managed

to file the humiliating incident away until that evening when she changed clothes and saw the bruise forming on her thigh. That explained the dull throb every time she put her weight on that leg. Instead of letting the minor injury interfere with her plan to have fun after getting Slade's apology over with, she donned a clean pair of jeans and her favorite sweatshirt. In a simple design that said it all, the soft mauve depicted the white outline of a human hand and dog paw in a high-five gesture.

She babied Sam a little, gave him a chew bone, and left for the club, positive all would go well and as planned tonight.

*****

What the fuck was I thinking? Grabbing my hastily packed bag off the motel bed that I'm fucking glad I'm not sleeping in tonight, I left the room and tossed it in the rental car's rear seat. Leaving without accomplishing my mission doesn't sit well but can't be helped, not after my hasty, faulty judgment upon seeing the bitch pop up out of the blue like that. I've never given in to temptation simply out of convenience, and this is the reason. Too much can go wrong and screw up everything else, such as well-laid-out plans. Driving back to the private airstrip, I went over new plans for a return trip in another few weeks. Despite the asinine last-second decision that ended in failure and possibly put Wells on alert, not returning to finish this isn't an option.

I never expected to see Nicole Wells there, not when I have yet to find where she's living. Somewhere near the highway strip mall didn't cut it with so much barren, open land everywhere I can see, the main thoroughfare only two lanes, and the numerous dirt road turnoffs unmarked. I'd hoped to finish this once and for all, quick and easy, and return home in time for the weekly family meeting. Now, I have to hurry back before anyone realizes I'm gone and then plan another trip to bumfuck Wyoming to end Wells' miserable existence. Next time around, though, I'll put the hunting skills our father taught us to use.

I have to do it for my peace of mind if nothing else. Family first, always. Dad also insisted on that.

****

"Have another, then we'll talk you into it." Allie slid her second beer across the table to Nicole. "My donation to the cause."

"*You* will talk her into it, not me. I think it's nuts to ride that thing." Lily feigned a shudder, glancing at the mechanical bull rocking in full motion, the rider laughing while getting tossed back and forth.

Nicole took a long pull on the brew before saying, "Thanks, I'll take the drink but pass on bull riding for now. I think it'll be easier to lose my riding virginity getting on a nice, calm, *small* horse first. And that ends your cause."

The mechanical bull looked fun, and she wanted to try it, but her leg was too sore to risk further bruising. She'd managed to slip inside Casey's an hour ago and hide her discomfort as she wound her way through the crowd to the table where Allie and Lily were already seated. Since then, she'd been ignoring Slade over at the bar while working on her apology.

"I get the gentler approach when it comes to losing your virginity, but after that pesky barrier is breached, there's something to be said for taking a walk on the wilder side. Which means finding a new cause to lead you astray on." Allie's eyes twinkled, her impish grin hard to resent, even when she jerked a thumb toward Slade.

"I have to agree with you there, and add, Nicole, that all three brothers are worth risking the ride."

Nicole put a hand to her brow with an exaggerated groan. "Lily, not you too. Allie's the one who likes to play matchmaker. I thought you were on my side, or at least neutral."

"Sorry, couldn't resist."

She couldn't suppress a chuckle, or her appreciation for their friendship. The opening tempted her to tell them she had already taken that risk with Slade, but she didn't dare hand over that ammunition.

Regardless of continuing to lust for the guy, proven again when her blood warmed upon seeing him again tonight, she didn't want another relationship. Not even a friends-with-benefits relationship.

Putting the one-night stand last weekend aside, the neighbors had welcomed her with food, assistance, and friendship, each visit chinking away at her belief she would heal faster if left alone. Without her realizing it, they'd quickly filled the void of missing her parents and friends back home, even though she had yet to reach out to Allie and Lily first. She would start there to deter them from matchmaking.

"If you have time, I'd love to try riding *a nice horse* this weekend. The contractors will keep me busy all next week."

"I have time," they said together.

"Wear a light coat. It's always colder out on the range until we reach a forest trail. Then you'll miss the sun though. By the way, love your shirt," Allie said.

"You'll have to tell us where to get something similar for Slade. He thinks we don't notice he's a softie for Chase."

Nicole believed Lily as he was a difficult man to read. "I'll send you the link." Now, though, she wanted to get an apology out of the way so she could find a dance partner able to defuse her growing hunger for tonight to end upstairs with Slade again. "Excuse me a minute."

She stood and meandered through the crowd toward the restrooms to divert the girls' attention, cursing when she couldn't help catching a glimpse of Slade on her way. He still wore his Stetson, which added mystery to the whole sexy, brooding cowboy image, and she wasn't the only one looking. Nicole noticed how women hung around the bar, some trying to engage him in small talk, which he appeared to ignore. She liked his *I don't give a shit* attitude when he walked away from their blatant flirting.

Maybe too much.

Kicking herself for that thought, she quit procrastinating and used the restroom. A quick apology, shake hands, and resist the tingles his touch would set off then get on with having the fun she promised herself. That was her plan until she stepped out and saw his usual detached expression soften as he greeted a tall, attractive blonde. Her heart tripped with an unexpected clutch in her abdomen as she stood rooted in place, witnessing the light kiss and their exit together, hand-in-hand, out the front door. Were they headed upstairs to that decadent room where Slade's undivided attention had been on her last week? Maybe on the same couch or bed where his every touch offered a reprieve from the months of constant guilt and regret.

It was a meaningless one-night stand, she repeated to herself before her imagination could picture them writhing together. And hadn't he just proven that? So she fantasized about a do-over after seeing him here again. He'd whetted her appetite for sex after a long drought — that's all the painful spasm meant. She didn't want another man in her life any more than he cared to get involved. Which didn't explain the pressure on her chest and the one eye on the door as she returned to the table.

Annoyed with herself and Slade for the slump in her mood, Nicole took her purse from Lily and called it a night. "Sorry. I'm tired and going home. What time tomorrow? What?" she demanded when they exchanged a look she couldn't decipher.

Allie never minced words. "There's nothing serious between Slade and Deb, the woman you saw him with. They've been close friends for years."

"And he's a great guy once you get to know him," Lily added.

Their assumption she was interested in Slade rubbed salt into the wound of her uncalled-for reaction and put her on the defensive. "First, I'm not blind, they're more than friends, and second, I don't care because I mind my own business." Okay, that came out bitchy, which she regretted right away. "I'm sorry. With all I have going on, I shouldn't have come out tonight."

Lily jumped up and hugged her, the move as unexpected as the lump forming in her throat. "No, no, we shouldn't have said anything." She pulled away, asking, "You'll still come tomorrow, won't you?"

"Please. Around eleven?" Allie pled.

"Sure. It was my idea, after all."

She looked forward to riding as much as she did to getting home tonight to gather her wits. They seem to have scattered in every direction possible. After saying good night, she wasted no time dashing out the door without paying attention until she ran into a wide chest and strong hands clasped her upper arms to steady her. The chill from leaving the warm interior for the colder night air dissipated the second she glanced up at Slade.

"Whoa. Going so soon? You weren't here long."

Nicole couldn't tell anything by his tone, which galled her since he was so adept at reading her, and she spoke without thinking. "Watching me while waiting for someone else. Tacky, Slade."

He dropped his hands and stood back. "You know what's said when you make assumptions, Nicole."

Wincing from another spasm of guilt, she watched him walk inside without another word or glance. *I really know how to screw up an evening out.* Nicole got in her car wondering where his friend had gone then drove home resigned to a long, sleepless night.

194

Chapter Nine

Slade slammed around his kitchen the next morning, taking his foul mood out on the coffee maker and toaster. When Chase wandered back to the bedroom instead of hanging around, begging for leftovers, he took a deep breath, stretched, and exhaled. He tried not to fault Nicole for jumping to conclusions, had spent the restless night making excuses for her misconceptions regarding his last visit and meeting with Deb last night. As soon as she'd arrived at Casey's, he wanted her with an ache that refused to go away. She managed to defuse his plan to haul her off to someplace quiet and set her straight. Right now, he wanted nothing more than to see where they might go with the attraction neither one could deny any longer.

Deb had made it easy by ending their

sexual relationship first, and he was happy for his longtime friend for finding someone who completed her in all ways. Even though their friends-with-benefits relationship had suited their needs for several years, he wouldn't sleep with one woman while he was so drawn toward someone else.

While running through options for his next visit to Nicole, he scrambled eggs then called Chase to join him for breakfast. "There," he said as the collie trotted toward his bowl. "Eggs. Am I forgiven?" The dog replied by chowing down and ignoring him. Slade sat at the table, confident Chase would forgive him now. There were too many irrefutable facts lining up for him to continue dismissing his interest in Nicole, he thought while eating. The compulsion to see her again despite her attitude; his inability to hold back when faced with her vulnerability last week at Casey's; the days and nights plagued by a sexual itch their night together had failed to scratch; the anger rippling through him instead of his usual indifference toward those whose opinions weren't supposed to matter.

Chase nudged his arm as he took his last

bite, those observant eyes glued to his final sausage link. "I'll trade your advice for the sausage."

"If he answers, I'm having you both committed," Brett said, walking in and making himself at home pouring a cup of coffee.

"I might go without a fight, given my mood. What brings you over so early?" he asked, storing his plate in the dishwasher.

Leaning against the counter, Brett eyed him over the cup, taking a sip before replying, "I need your help bringing in the horses from the north pasture. The guys didn't show up this morning."

Shit. "None of them?" The college kids were part-time and rotated on weekends, which gave their full-time employees days off. When one couldn't make it, they would trade off together.

"Nope. No calls, either. I didn't bother checking with either Keith or Riley, who were scheduled. Allie and Lily are taking Nicole riding before that cold snap comes in later today, so I want to get back to choose her mount, and Reed has already left to help at the shelter."

Well, that settled his plans. Now there was no time to drop in on Nicole for a much-needed talk, not with the morning and early afternoon taken assisting Brett, returning home to deal with the hands in private, and then leaving for Sunday dinner with their mom afterward. The only positive spin on the day was hearing about Nicole's effort to socialize. The biggest negative was missing out on the privilege of teaching her to ride, his disappointment in the college hires a close second.

"Finish that, and let's get going. We're not riding far, so we'll bring Chase."

They made good time even with stopping to check on one of the oil wells, the ranch's main income source. With Chase's herding, the mustangs stayed close and moved at a steady pace, their sensitivity to weather changes also helping to move them along. Slade drove back to his place not happy about the next chore on his list. He'd much rather be riding out with Nicole for a frank talk than deciding whether to fire Keith and Riley. One thing was a given; he was fucking tired of dealing with their irresponsibility and ready to put an end to the destructive pranks of the last year. Which meant the possibility of letting Evan go also, whom he suspected was behind the damaging behavior, and then losing Jeff, who wouldn't stay on without his friends.

Not how he cared to end the weekend or start the long cold winter.

Slade drove home with his mind on the employees, unprepared for a surprise visit from Nicole. His pulse quickened, an immediate reaction he'd come to expect whenever he clapped eyes on her, always followed by a strong sexual pull that exceeded his previous experiences. Those telltale signs were the reason he decided to push himself and her into more. He parked and opened the door, waiting for Chase to hop down before closing it and facing her as she strode forward. Her flannel-lined denim jacket flapped open wide enough to read the bold black lettering on her yellow top – *If My Dog Doesn't Like You We Can't Be Friends.* No doubt Sam liked him, and, despite the shadows under her eyes, the rueful grin teasing the corners of her mouth gave him hope she was more open-minded today.

"Lily mentioned your place was the third house when I joined them for lunch at Allie's. Here." She thrust a Rubbermaid container at him. "Snickerdoodle cookies from scratch with my apology."

Not one to pass up a good opportunity or olive branch, he took the cookies with one hand and cupped her nape with the other. Hauling her against him, he covered her gaping mouth with his. The pleasure of her soft lips yielding under his went straight to his groin, that supple body quivering against throwing him into a tailspin of aggressive need he struggled to control. To hell with dealing with irresponsible college kids. He'd much rather spend the time doing this. She opened under his assault, and he raided her mouth with tongue and teeth, every slide of her lips against his, each matching tongue stroke, the taste of her soft gums just as he remembered. He eased up before the temptation to push for more put his intentions at risk.

Slade lifted his head, retaining his hold

as he said, "I'll accept both if you go riding with me instead of Allie and Lily."

"Oh, well." Nicole stepped back and he dropped his hand, amused by seeing her flustered for the first time. "That wouldn't be right."

"They not only won't mind, they'll be thrilled. Their goal in life is to see me take the fall like my brothers." Panic crossed her face and he rushed to set her at ease. "Relax. I'm only proposing a ride and an overdue talk."

The blunt, prickly neighbor resurfaced, and she squared her shoulders. "You want to discuss sex."

"Agree to ride with me and I'll let you know what I want. Besides, you owe me two apologies. Consider this the second."

"You play dirty."

"Sweetheart, you have no idea."

She looked over at Chase who lay in the grass. "Okay, if Allie and Lily are good with it. Can I pet your dog?"

"Chase." He pointed to Nicole. "Friend."

Slade set the cookies on the truck hood and pulled out his phone, watching Nicole smile as Chase danced around her, tail wagging faster when she talked to him. "Such a good boy, aren't you?"

As his dog ate up the attention, he sent a text to have Bandit saddled then talked to Allie. As he thought, she was only too happy for Nicole to go out with him instead. He hung up, pocketed the phone, and grabbed the cookies. "Allie said have a good time and they'll talk to you later. Ready?"

Her smile turned teasing. "Maybe now I'd rather play with Chase."

If dogs brought out her softer side, Slade doubted Chase would mind if he used him as bait. "You can introduce him and Sam together later. I have a family dinner in a few hours, so we need to get going."

*****

The time limit helped dispel Nicole's reservations about Slade's offer. She'd stopped by his place first hoping he'd greet her surprise visit and peace offering with gruff indifference, giving her a good excuse to keep her distance. Instead, he'd kissed her, damn it. With her lips tingling and pussy still fluttering, now all she could think about was a repeat of his sexual brand for relieving stress. Between changing the plans for the shelter and Natalie's renewed harassment, she could use a few hours of mind-numbing orgasmic bliss again. She could delve into what appeared to be an irrefutable weakness when he touched her later.

I really read him wrong, she admitted as he held the truck door open for her. Nicole got in, regretting even more jumping to the wrong conclusion about Slade's motive for visiting last weekend and walking out with that woman last night. She was lucky he was so willing to spend time with her and looking forward to riding. Maybe not today since he had a family obligation, but sometime soon, she hoped her olive branch was enough for a repeat of those hours upstairs at Casey's. And that's all she wanted, that short respite from missing the connection she'd shared with Tony.

After letting Chase in the back seat, he pulled out of the drive, saying, "It's a few miles to the stables and barns. While you're in such an agreeable mood, why don't you tell me about the assault that left that scar."

The out-of-the-blue request, stated in his usual matter-of-fact tone, caught her off guard. She paused in rubbing Chase's chin before rallying enough to respond with her standard answer. "Because I don't talk about it. How much of this state do you own anyway?"

He cut her a brief glance, but his lowered hat brim once again hid his expression. "A good portion, which you don't care about. We've been naked together. You should be able to discuss the incident that led you there."

"How do you know I don't care about your worth?" she shot back, grateful he hadn't mentioned how she'd begged him to fuck her.

"Because it takes a great deal of money to do what you're doing." Holding the steering wheel steady on the dirt road with one hand, he rubbed his jaw with the other. Staring straight ahead, he said, "I was trained as a military sniper and spent two years in Afghanistan. I've killed to save others, once to save myself, and yet, guilt and uncertainty still hit me after each one."

Nicole stepped through the open door he held, oddly receptive to the invitation now that he'd revealed his vulnerability. "How did you get over it?" she asked as the dark-red, white-trimmed ranch buildings came into view.

"It took time to stop questioning whether there was another way. I kept reminding myself I acted in self-defense of others." Slade parked in front of an enormous stable, the wide doors slid open to reveal a few hired hands moving about inside. Opening his door, he said, "Wait, and I'll help you down."

She waited, but only because his touch would distract her from the warm fuzzy she experienced whenever his tone exuded concern for her ordeal, never forgetting his anger on her behalf the first time he noticed the scar. Only her parents and closest friends distressed over her trauma, never blaming her in words or expression. None of Tony's siblings had asked how she was or expressed remorse for what she'd suffered, too worried about the publicity, what went into the papers, and holding up their good name for both business and social standing.

Slade grasped her waist under her open jacket and lifted her off the seat, holding her long enough to stabilize the rise of unplanned emotions. Then he clasped her hand, tugging her around the side of the stable toward a corral, stirring her libido this time. She sucked in a lungful of chilly air, which helped her regain her perspective. *Sexual chemistry, that's all that's brewing between them.* She spotted only one horse, a striking tan stallion with black mane and tail, tethered and saddled.

"Thanks, Barry," he told the younger ranch hand. "Sorry you were called in today. I'll see it doesn't happen again. Double-time pay."

"It was no problem, boss, but I appreciate that. Christmas will be here before we know it. Ma'am." Barry tipped his hat to her before leaving them alone.

Scowling at Slade, she stated, "I'm not old enough to be called ma'am, and why one horse?" She eyed the huge stallion with trepidation.

"Your first time will be easier riding with me." Taking the reins, he swung into the saddle and reached a hand down. "Trust me if you want to go."

Put like that, she couldn't refuse. She'd been looking forward to this outing too much. Taking his hand, she found herself hoisted up and settled in front of him before she could take a breath. She shivered, a combination of cold, anticipation, and awareness, his arms coming around and securing her from toppling off as they started out. To calm her jitters, she stretched an arm to stroke the stallion's arched, soft neck.

"What's his name?"

"Bandit."

"That fits. *Oh*," she sighed softly, the view from this height breathtaking. She could see across the vast expanse of fields to the far-off mountain silhouette, enough wooded forest running along both sides to add a touch of green to the landscape.

"I never tire of it. Is this and your shelter worth leaving the big city behind, along with your friends and family?"

He had a way of tossing out a personal

inquiry when she least expected it, usually on the heels of a generic statement, but this one she didn't mind answering. "I don't regret it yet. And I've changed my mind about the shelter and plan to foster instead. The Casper shelter's director seemed pleased with my offer."

"Marilyn is good with people and animals. Lean against me and hold on to the pommel or my arms." He tapped a thumb on the protruding knob between her thighs. Slade wouldn't admit it, but he was good with people also.

Nicole gripped the pommel with one hand and his forearm with the other, then he nudged Bandit into a trot that swayed her against his chest and arms despite her hold. The stallion's smooth stride enabled Slade to bend close to her ear when he spoke, pointing out where he and his brothers used to run wild and get into trouble. She enjoyed the tingles from his warm breath as much as riding close to several bison and the graceful swoop of soaring eagles. They halted at a lake where an elk continued to drink as Bandit dipped his head on the opposite side.

Twisting around, she gazed up at him, relishing the warmth of his big body shielding her from the cold breeze. "That was fun. Thank you."

"You're welcome." He turned Bandit around, and she faced forward as they started the trek back. When he spoke, he picked up where he'd left off in the truck, once again catching her off guard. "It took me way too long to realize I couldn't put my actions in the military behind me until I forgave myself. You won't be able to, either, until you forgive yourself for taking his life."

Because he was the only person she'd met who might possibly understand, she told him what she'd never admitted to anyone else. It was easier not facing him, though. "That's not what I can't forgive. He loved me. Truly. Deeply. The real deal everyone wants but that I couldn't return. I mean, I loved him, cared more than I ever had before but wasn't *in* love with him." She gave him a brief rundown of Tony's inoperable, malignant tumor then fingered her scar, saying, "He wasn't in his right mind, and I thought I was doing the right thing ignoring the doctor's warnings to give him more time at home, surrounded by familiarity. I was wrong."

He clasped her chin, turned her head around, then thumbed his hat up enough to snag her undivided attention with his direct gray gaze. "Punishing yourself doesn't change his diagnosis, or the inevitable outcome. I get how you felt about him as it sounds similar to my feelings for Deb, the woman you saw me walk out with last night. We're not in love but have enjoyed a special friendship that included an occasional hookup for bondage play without either of us expecting or desiring more. Right before you came out, we agreed to take that off the table, her because she'd grown serious about someone, and me because my thoughts are more on you than anyone else lately."

She should not feel good about that candid revelation and went with her first inclination to defuse the warm fuzzy, pouncing on what else he'd said. "You use the term hookup instead of relationship. What does that say about you?"

"That when I do end up in a relationship, there will be no hookups for either one of us."

That potent look accompanied his compelling statement, the combination producing a ripple of longing she wasn't ready to consider. Swiveling forward, she asked, "Can we ride fast?"

"Sure." Wrapping an arm around her waist, he held her snug against his chest and kicked Bandit into an all-out run, the exhilarating rush robbing her of breath.

More of these euphoric experiences, that's all Nicole swore she wanted from Slade as the trees and ground sped by in a blur and his muscled strength sheltered her from the cold. Wild rides or wild sex – she would take either if it resulted in such pleasure of the senses as long as her heart remained unaffected.

*****

Nicole tried to hide her pleased relief when Slade explained his and Deb's relationship, but he'd become adept at reading her. As they neared the stables, he reined Bandit to a trot and took advantage of holding her close with no complaint to keep the momentum going his way.

Bending to her ear, he tugged the small lobe with his teeth, savoring the telltale way she arched sideways to offer better access. "Now that we've cleared the air, are you ready to admit we should explore what's brewing between us?"

"Sex only?" she asked with a small catch in her voice.

"For starters."

She remained quiet as they rode into the stable yard and he dismounted. Holding his arms up, he plucked her from the saddle, not risking letting her move away from him yet. She was more receptive to him when they were touching. When she leaned in to him, he felt her legs tremble, either from the ride or his suggestion.

"What would you do if I said yes?"

Their short history taught him not to wait if she was in an amiable frame of mind. Grabbing a hand, he pulled her toward the stable after verifying no one else was around. "I'm better at showing than telling," he stated, making sure it was empty inside then hurrying into the tack room that doubled as an office, the only space with a door.

She gasped then frowned, scanning the room. "Now, in here?"

"Here you go with the now question." Slade backed her against the door and pressed her lips in a deep kiss, controlling her mouth while loosening her jeans until she went lax and breathed a warm sigh into his mouth. Her rapid embracement was the same as before, and the exact reception he'd been hoping for.

Slipping a hand between their waists, he paused with his middle finger poised at the apex of her already damp slit and lifted his head. "Got a problem with here and now?"

"Nope, none at all."

Relishing the lack of hesitation, he found her clit and played with the distended nub. He'd learned not to give her the time and space to change her mind. "We have to be quick," he warned.

"I like quick."

"I remember." Encouraged, Slade drew her to the small corner desk and bent her over. "Brace yourself."

"I remember," she quipped, likely referring to her tight grip of his arms the last time.

He pushed her jeans down, appreciating her rare humor, then saw the large bruise covering half of her thigh. Running his fingers lightly over the purple skin, he asked, "What happened?"

Nicole went still and kept her face forward, two suspicious reactions to the simple inquiry. "A clumsy mishap. What happened to quick?" She wiggled her enticing bare butt.

"Seeing you hurt distracted me." He fished out a condom and released his cock, stifling his irritation. If he lectured her on holding back, she would just point out this was sex only, and he didn't want to hear that. Not when he was so close to admitting he was ready for more.

Unable to resist, he held her hips and slid inside her snug, slick heat, savoring the tight grip of her vaginal muscles clinging to his cock. Pausing, he swatted one cheek, her startled gasp and the red imprint against the creamy flesh enough to satisfy his annoyance with the way she kept bottled up. Hadn't he done the same thing only to regret holding his brothers' at arm's length for so long? The fewer disappointments she harbored going forward, the better.

"Why did you do that?" She turned to gaze at him with confusion instead of accusation.

"For keeping this"—he touched the bruise—"from me." Her pussy clenched as he withdrew slowly, her eyes going dark before she swung around with a low groan.

"Slade."

The entreaty propelled him forward again, and latching onto her hip, he held her still for his steady assault into her creamy depths. Pumping with vigorous intent, he wished they didn't have to rush, enjoying the snug fit of their bodies, her soft cries, and straining body even more this time around. Not surprised, he worked her into a state of desperate need within moments, her hands fisting as she laid her forehead down. He sucked in a deep breath, striving for control when her pussy rippled around his cock, loving her fast response to his jackhammering possession. The desk shifted as he strove to join her in climax, her orgasm aiding his efforts, making it easier to fuck her harder, faster until he erupted with a heavy grunt.

*****

The orgasm ripped into Nicole with sharp tentacles of such pleasure it bordered on pain. Nerve endings flared to life, and her slick muscles clutched around the thick flesh stretching and burning her tight pussy. *Why him, why now?* she kept asking herself as she struggled to regain an iota of sanity through the mind-numbing, body-encompassing euphoric frenzy consuming her. Once again, the sheer decadence of letting go with Slade, regardless of where or when, left her overwhelmed and floundering to come up with a reasonable explanation. Sex had always been easy, uncomplicated, and nice. Considering he wasn't the type she usually went for, these rendezvous were anything but.

The cool air wafting across her exposed buttocks wasn't enough to temper the heat from that spank or prevent the eye-opening, arousing effect from the sting. Her orgasm seemed to go on and on, the spasmodic clutches refusing to ease until he quivered inside her with his own release.

He loosened his grip on her cheeks, and an image of finger indents on her buttocks popped in her head. There was no point denying she relished every second of his tight hold or the hot rush from her inability to move. There was something freeing about submitting to his sexual dominance. Her only regret came from missing the feel of his naked body against hers, his damp warm skin stretched over taut, bulging muscles sliding over her.

Until he pulled out of her still-rippling sheath.

Straightening with Slade's assistance, Nicole found herself wishing they could linger a little longer. Not even the nearby voices filtering in from outside the stable changed that bothersome admission. She'd already betrayed Tony once by her inability to fall in love with him; she couldn't do so again by wanting anything more from a man this soon other than to appease the basic bodily function of lust.

"Come to dinner with me."

She reached for his arms as he pulled up her jeans and yanked her against him with a tug on the waist. "I can't. Thanks though." *I need space and perspective,* she thought, her face warming when she realized he hadn't even removed his hat.

Booted footfalls resonated from the stable's bricked aisle, and Slade hastened to right his clothing. "If you're sure, I'll take you back to get your car. Maybe I can change your mind on the way."

Chapter Ten

Chicago

66What were you thinking?" Michael tossed Natalie's phone back to her.

Picking it up off the white velvet sofa, she scowled at her pain-in-the-ass oldest brother. "I made it clear I won't let her get away with killing Tony." She should have known he would discover the threatening texts she'd been sending Nicole. "Douglas found her and her new number." She cut her glare over to Douglas who leaned with negligent insolence against the marble fireplace. The traitor had remained silent during Michael's tirade.

He shrugged with as much unconcern as he'd shown since Michael started laying into her the minute she stepped through the door. "I don't see the problem with a little harassment. It's fun to picture her reaction reading them."

Michael slammed his glass on the bar countertop. He seemed to do that a lot lately. "There's nothing amusing about those threats. They could result in charges."

"With our money? Not likely." If that was the only argument he could come up with, that wouldn't stop her. The bitch *would* pay. She would see to it.

"Relax, Michael. Wells lives out in the boonies, from what I can figure of her location. I doubt there's anyone around who will give a fig about her problems back home. Let sis have her fun."

Douglas smiled at her, daring her to mention his involvement. Natalie wouldn't because she needed him, but he should remember she was good at getting revenge. "It's not fun. It's retribution."

"I don't care what you call it. Stop. Now," Michael ordered.

"No." She rose and stormed toward the door, tossing over her shoulder, "Cut my allowance. Hell, fire me if you choose. It won't stop me. Nothing will."

Natalie slammed out of the house before she gave in to the tears. She had adored Tony and their special bond. She'd told Nicole over and over she wanted to be there for him, especially during his last weeks. He died in her arms, by her hand, and she didn't have it in her to let that go.

*****

Slade failed to persuade Nicole to join them for Sunday dinner, so to distract him from that disappointment, he brought Chase to play with Brandy. And with luck, their antics would distract Lily and Allie from mentioning his outing with Nicole. His mother would appreciate it if Chase wore out her high-energy goldendoodle, but would love as much to hear he'd taken a serious interest in a woman. How serious depended on whether Nicole kept an open mind going forward. At least she'd agreed to think about it when he'd dropped her off.

He took his time driving to Eagle's Nest, contemplating whether he should even bother, but there it was, that little twinge whenever he considered backing off. She'd taken the first move earlier in extending her apology, an encouraging sign even though she'd turned down his invite. He understood the confusion of their mutual attraction and her reluctance to enter into another full-fledged relationship.

"However," he stated aloud, glancing at Chase as he parked at his parents' house. "If I can risk that leap, so can she. It's not as if she isn't interested." Chase barked and pawed the door. "Mind out of the gutter, buddy. Brandy's been fixed."

Slade held the door open for him and they went straight into the back yard. Willow came barreling out the dog door when she saw Chase, and he took advantage of their romping to slip inside the house through the slider.

"The dogs are tearing up your yard." He kissed his mother's cheek after hanging up his hat and jacket. "They love the cooler weather." As he'd hoped, Lily and Allie's attention went from chopping vegetables at the kitchen counter to looking out the window above the sink and laughing.

"I'm glad you brought Chase. Now we won't need to walk her after dinner. Your brothers and William are watching football."

The joy his mother reaped from their family Sunday dinners always shone in Andrea's sparkling green eyes. Whether expressing happiness, disappointment, or displeasure, one look was all it ever took to ensure he and his brothers would yield to her wishes.

"Holler when you want the dogs to settle down before coming inside."

"They're fine. Dinner in fifteen."

Taking advantage of the girls' continued distraction, he didn't linger and strode into the den. A small fire crackled in the corner fireplace, the extra warmth adding to the cozy room. William rose from the sofa and handed Slade the opened beer sitting on the bar cart. "Score's seven to seven, two minutes left in the fourth."

"Mom won't hold dinner or allow football during, so one better end it in that time," he said, opting to take the recliner with a drink holder on the arm.

"How was your ride?"

From the expectation reflected in Reed's tone, he wasn't surprised one or both of the girls had told his brothers about the last-minute switch. Since his stepfather's attention was on the game, Slade leaned forward and lowered his voice. "Please tell me they haven't mentioned it to Mom."

Brett grinned but William answered without taking his eyes off the television. "You would still be upstairs getting grilled if they had. Heard tell someone moved in out there at the Studman's old place."

"That's all we told him after we came downstairs. Intercepted! Well, shit. There goes ten bucks." Brett pulled out his wallet and handed the money to their stepfather as the game ended with a field goal.

"Then keep it that way. I don't want her planning my wedding during dinner."

"She's not that bad. Come on. Let's eat before the next game starts."

Thirty minutes later, Slade leaned back in his chair, feeling good. As usual, his mother's cooking and family relaxed him. That didn't keep his mind off Nicole or the details she'd revealed about the assault that left her scarred inside and out. Glancing around the table, he could only imagine the difficulty of making those decisions with a loved one. Now he understood what had driven her to leave home and family and why she'd wanted solitude.

Speaking of family – wouldn't they all love to know how entrenched he'd become in Nicole, and not only with her well-being. He couldn't recall wanting a woman with such intensity, or one he couldn't move on from without regrets or stop thinking about, itching to learn more every time he saw her.

Did he love her?

Across from Slade, Reed sat next to Lily, his arm draped over the back of her chair, fingers idly stroking her shoulder as he idly conversed with William on his opposite side. While passing the pork chop platter and vegetable bowls around the table, Brett would take each from Allie with a lingering touch on her hand or wrist. Subtle nuances that were so common now between the couples, even his mother had stopped noticing.

It was too soon to answer his question because he wouldn't settle for less than what his brothers and mother now shared with their significant others. But he was closer than he'd ever been, and that told him something significant was developing with Nicole.

Allie leaned around Brett to look at him, her blue eyes alit with amusement, and he braced for what he knew she would say.

"How did Nicole like riding with you today?"

Damn. And here he'd believed he would get out of here keeping that tidbit from his mother a little longer.

"Nicole?" Andrea, seated at the head of the table, laid her hand on his forearm with a beaming smile. "Who's that, dear?"

"Our new neighbor, Nicole Wells, and don't go making more of it than giving her a riding lesson and showing her around, Mom."

"Oh! Thank goodness she's okay and well enough to ride. William and I were so worried when she refused to go to the hospital after that car hit her in the mercantile parking lot. I didn't know she was the one who bought the Studman place."

Slade stiffened and went cold inside, recalling with vivid clarity Nicole's bruised thigh. Anger and concern over her evasive duplicity when he'd ask her about it roiled inside his gut.

"She didn't mention it. What happened?" he asked, noticing everyone else's worry.

"Damnedest thing," William replied with a frown. "Idiot driver came speeding out of one of the rows then down the front of the restaurant and store. You'd think the hounds of hell were hot on his heels. I didn't take the chance she could move fast enough and was right there. We both landed on the ground, and she favored her leg when she insisted she was fine and walked to her car. She wouldn't hear of getting checked out though. Seemed uncomfortable with the crowd and attention."

"She didn't say a word when we made plans to take her out today. We should go over there tomorrow, Allie." Lily's voice reflected her constant compassion for others.

"Excuse me." Slade had heard enough from William's account. "Sorry to eat and run. Thanks, Mom, William." He strode out without another word. None of them would expect further explanation anyway.

Irrational outrage churned inside him as he called to Chase and left through the backyard. It defied common sense to blame himself for not being there to protect Nicole against harm, to compare saving complete strangers using prewarned intel to blasting himself when someone he cared about was hurt when he lacked that prior knowledge. And whether he should or should not be so put out with her for not telling him, he was, and he made no excuses for that, driving to her place.

Stars lit up the night sky by the time he parked in front of her house, his blood still pumping hot enough to fend off the drop in temperature when he strode to the door and rapped loudly.

"Why did you lie to me?" he demanded the minute she opened the door. Shoving past her, he waited only long enough for her to close the door before pinning her against it with one hand braced against the wood, the other cupping her nape, caging her in with his body. "A car damn near ran you down. That. Is. Not. A clumsy mishap."

Nicole's surprise at seeing Slade changed to a narrow-eyed glare. "Maybe because it's none of your business."

He traced the rapid pulse in her neck with his thumb. If the color suffusing her face stemmed just from anger and her eyes weren't dilated, her breathing so shallow, he would back off. Instead, he let loose with the dominant urgency to take control, finally daring to give her what she was silently asking for and didn't realize she needed.

"*You* are my business, have been ever since you begged me over"—he bent and nipped the tender skin on her neck—"and over." He slid his lips up to her ear and bit the small lobe, whispering, "And over." Releasing her, he gazed into her eyes, saw the acceptance she wasn't quite ready to admit, and snatched her hand. "You should have told me," he admonished, flinging his jacket and hat off before taking a seat on the three-piece modular sectional.

"What are you doing?"

Her voice hitched as he reached out to loosen her jeans and yanked them down. Tugging her over his lap, he delivered one swat to her cheek, enough for a minimal sting, with luck, enough to entice instead of reject. Pausing, Slade rested a hand on the pink spot. "Yes or no, Nicole."

"Yes." *Please.* Nicole had no choice when she thought about it, jerking when Slade smacked her bare butt again. Either Slade's commanding concern or the twinging burn soothed the conflicting emotions she'd battled all evening. She returned home earlier hoping out

of sight would put him and the yearnings he also pulled to the forefront out of mind.

No such luck.

A groan escaped her clenched throat with the next spank, this one a little harder, stinging, the heat seeping into muscle. She questioned how she could allow this, lie here and ache for another distracting, hurtful swat. Then it came, landing on the opposite buttock, resulting in a twin response. Instead of adding to the tension plaguing her for one reason or another over this odd relationship she had going with the neighbor, she slowly relaxed under his steadily descending hand.

"This is for lying."

Slade's hand came down even harder on the under curve of one cheek, eliciting a soft startled cry and catching her off guard enough to wiggle from the impact. He aimed for the other side next, the tip of one finger grazing her slit, her damp arousal swift, as hot as her butt.

"Slade," Nicole moaned, her brain going numb, much like her butt when he peppered both cheeks with quick, sharp slaps.

"That's my girl," she heard him say through the roaring in her head and coming to terms with the arousing effects of this painful, somewhat mortifying act.

The praise added to the pleasure/pain encompassing her body, her nipples peaking from rubbing back and forth on the sofa, her palms and forehead sweating as she kept her face downward. Thank goodness he had held her legs still pinned under one of his, his free hand a comforting pressure between her shoulders. Then he halted the torment with an abruptness that snagged her already ragged breathing and eased the discomfort of her throbbing backside with slow caresses over the tender skin. A shiver rippled under her skin, one of pleasure and serenity, a feeling that brought a sheen to her eyes.

Nicole's sudden vulnerability threatened to send her into full-panic mode, but Slade caught her before she could struggle off his lap. Flipping her upright, he wrapped those thick, strong arms around her and held tight, leaving her no option but to bury her face in his shoulder and let the dam burst. She couldn't say why, and not because her butt hurt, or that the abrasive bare skin contact with his denim-clad thighs brought her to the edge of a humiliating climax.

So awash with the bombardment of conflicting responses to his heavy hand, she barely registered his hand sliding between her legs, his finger finding her clit, or the small tugs on the tender nub until he spoke. "Go over for me, baby." His lips were soft against her ear, his voice rough. Tingling. Heat producing. She should despise that generic pet name, but instead, relished the way it kept this scene where she needed it, without involving the deeper emotion, teary breakdown threatened.

Tightening her hand in his shirt, Nicole caved to the demanding arousal Slade was so damn good at producing. With her jeans still restricting her thigh spread, she arched into his busy hand, the pressure of his palm against her pubis coupled with deep, clit-abrasive finger thrusts enough to release orgasm. She splintered on a shrill cry, the pleasure just as sweeping, body-encompassing as always, regardless or because of the discomfort she ached with remaining undecided.

He didn't wait for her head to clear completely before talking again. "It was my last assignment in Afghanistan, and I couldn't wait to go home and put the killing behind me. I'd carried out seven executions already, regretted the necessity but not the deaths. They were evil, pure and simple, each one. Even the one woman. And I saved countless lives. I figure that saves me when it comes to any moral objectiveness."

He paused and she held her breath, not

needing to hear more but owing him enough to listen to everything.

"I didn't know until he was dead and turned over. A kid. I later learned he'd been abducted and forced through torture and threats to his family who were in another village. Nine years old; the fucking bastards couldn't do their own dirty work. Not even a unit's success of taking them out helped ease the guilt."

Nicole pushed hard against his snug embrace and looked up at him. "I'm sorry you have to live with that." Her own experience allowed her to hurt for him.

Slade stood with her in his arms and took long strides to the hall, asking with rough gruffness, "Which room?"

"Second on the right."

He dropped her on the bed, and they both stripped in haste and silence. Instead of coming together in frenzied need again, they took it slow – hands gliding over perspiration-damp flesh, lips taking turns suckling nipples, teeth sinking into sensitive, nerve-laden spots – stoking the fire until a blazing heat quickened the pace. Slade flipped her over, yanked her to her knees, and powered inside her quivering sheath until the inferno consumed them both. Nicole rolled over with a sigh and fell into a contented sleep, the first in countless months.

*****

Slade awoke alone then found Nicole outside with the dogs, a cup of coffee in one hand, deleting what appeared to be a text with the other. She glanced up at his approach, her cheeks rosy from the chilly air as she stuck the phone in her jacket pocket. He let her speak first, having a pretty good idea what was going on in that head of hers.

"You have to go. The contractors are coming. And Paul."

He recognized the shield she put up as a defense mechanism against feelings she hadn't plan for. *Welcome to the club, sweetheart.* The military taught him when to push forward and when to retreat. It didn't sit well in this instance to go with the latter, but he won last night's battle and wouldn't push his luck when he intended to win the war.

"So I do." He took the cup from her hand and drank, keeping his eyes on her as he handed it back. Leaning down, he kissed her, quick as he didn't trust himself to stop there. "I'll call." Whistling for Chase, he didn't give her the option to reply before pivoting and rounding the house to reach the truck.

Checking the time, Slade switched mental gears and drove straight to the barn where the guys were scheduled to work this morning. Normally, he enjoyed interacting with his employees, having developed an easy rapport and friendship with all except the college part-time hires. When he first hired them, he'd hoped one or two would stay on, fill vacancies he had kept open. Now, instead of offering them the full-time positions when they graduated, they would be lucky to hold on to their current employment or get a referral from him.

Chase followed him inside the barn and ran over to Evan for the attention he knew he would get. All four paused in stacking hay bales, Evan bending to rub Chase behind the ears, his dog's favorite spot.

"None of you are stupid. You're well aware we have a problem." Hands on hips, he slid his glower from one to the other. "Enough, Evan. Pay attention, or I'll dock your final pay for this morning's time and kick you out now."

Evan straightened, the fondness he always showed for Chase and the horses changing to the familiar belligerence he saved for him and his brothers. Slade should have recognized that red flag from the beginning, as well as a few other telltale clues, if his suspicions proved true.

"I'm done punishing you for poor behavior and work ethics. You're not kids. Either you agree to switch your hours to working ten on Saturdays and six on Sunday afternoons, no more weekdays, no weekends off, or you're fired."

From the panic and anger on their shocked faces, they weren't expecting such stern repercussions. Even though they now put in time on weekends, they rotated hours and days, leaving them plenty of time to party and study. Ten-hour days of physical labor were exhausting, even for younger people.

"That's not fair," Jeff protested then turned on Evan. "Didn't you ask them to switch with us for tomorrow?" He pointed to Keith and Riley.

"I may have forgotten." Evan surprised Slade when he said, "I'll work alone Saturdays. Let them off."

Guilt could work wonders, he mused, hearing the change from insolence to sincerity in Evan's words. But until he got to the truth about the vandalism, he wouldn't let him off the hook. "Put in your two hours this morning and finish stacking the hay. I'll let you all know before next weekend." He hoped the pressure of waiting for his friends' fate would prompt him to come clean about everything else as he walked out.

Chapter Eleven

"Are you sure you want to start staying here?" Nicole asked Paul as they crossed the yard to the cottage. Jim Baker arrived first thing this morning with his crew, and Paul had shown up not long afterward appearing cautiously optimistic about taking this step. She understood grief and still couldn't imagine getting through the depth of his loss.

"It's ten times better than anyplace I've bedded down in a long time." He eyed the small barn-shaped quarters with appreciation.

"Well, like I said, the heat works well. They went ahead and updated the plumbing in the bath and kitchen this morning, and replaced the commode and vanity while they were at it." She opened the door, closing it against the cold breeze as soon as they got inside, and waved a hand toward the kitchenette. "I still want to have the cabinets refinished and the countertop replaced. Only apartment-size appliances would fit, and, as you can see," she said, turning to face the opposite side of the single room, "there's just that half wall separating the sofa from the bed. At least the one window is large and gives you a nice view to wake up to." Other than a dresser and compact table with two chairs, no other furniture would fit in the eight-hundred-square-foot space. "Bathroom's here." She pointed to the one separate room behind her.

"It's perfect, and much appreciated." Paul held out his hand. "I'll go see where I can help your workers first and get settled this evening. It's not like I have much to unload from the car."

No, she figured he'd spent more effort coping with heartbreak than replacing the material possessions he'd lost while unemployed. Nicole wanted to baby him a little, talk him into relaxing for the two hours of daylight left, but she understood the need to keep the mind occupied with busy work.

"Jim can probably find a task for you. I'll leave you to it, then. Come to the house for dinner." She held up a hand when he started to protest. "I insist on including dinner in your benefits. I mostly fix casseroles that make plenty for two for three meals, so it's no big deal. You can eat here if you prefer. Trust me when I say I understand."

He swiveled toward the window with a jerky nod. "Thanks."

Nicole opened the door, saying, "Stop by when Jim's done, and I'll have it ready."

She left before his emotional duress rubbed off on her. After Slade had gone from taking her with the dominant aggression she loved to slow tenderness she'd responded to as easily, she was troubled by her own topsy-turvy feelings. Not to mention her shocking response to his hard hand on her bare butt. This morning, while she showered and dressed, she swore she could still feel leftover tingles from that hot discomfort racing across her tender flesh. Inhaling a deep breath of cool air, she forced those thoughts aside.

Her phone beeped with a text as she

strode toward the barn. Checking the sender, she pressed delete seeing Natalie's name again. Tolerance for Tony's twin's grief was one thing; allowing her to continue this constant harassment was another. She didn't want to cause trouble, but she would never attain the peace she'd come here to find if she didn't put an end to this.

Nicole entered the barn, tabling that decision until these renovations were done and she could consider the options with a clearer head. Of course, if Slade kept coming around, the clearer head might not ever return. How could a bad case of lust last so long? She had indulged in more sex with him in the last ten days than she had the previous ten months, yet she still went damp with one look, one simple touch.

Deranged Cowboy syndrome. Or insanity. There were no other explanations she could come up with.

"Wow, you move fast," she told Jim, her gaze scanning the insulated walls and cleared concrete floor.

"I have a good crew. Work moves faster without obstacles. Open spaces like this are easy unless we run into problems. So far, nothing I didn't already find on the inspection has popped up."

Six young men had worked up a sweat even in this cool interior. Nicole shivered inside her coat, nothing she wasn't used to. Growing up in the frigid Chicago winters with the wind blowing off the lake didn't mean she endured long cold months without complaint.

"The pups and I will enjoy the heat once it's in."

"You're paying a hefty amount to heat this place. Bedding them inside with hay would have saved you a lot. Just saying."

She shrugged. Investing Tony's money in the charity work that brought them together helped settle her conscience over inheriting from his suffering. The Renaldis didn't need it. Natalie resented her for it, but Nicole just added it to the list of other things she resented her for, like breathing.

"It's going to good use; that's all that matters. My new handyman is here already and wants to help if you wouldn't mind giving him something. Let's just say he needs busy work."

Jim patted her shoulder in a fatherly manner. "You're a good person, Nicole. I can find something for him. I have the heating contractor coming tomorrow. With luck, we'll have that going before the snow predicted at the end of the week. Planning on drywall and paint Wednesday, kennels and cleanup Thursday, maybe into Friday. The counters for the cottage will be in next week."

"Sounds good. I'll make a trip in to Casper midweek and stop at the shelter with an update. Thanks, Jim. See you in the morning."

Nicole brought Sam inside when she returned to the house. Ever since she'd made the mistake with the coyote, she hadn't left him out alone at dawn or dusk. She disliked owing Slade gratitude, yet she wouldn't discount his timely appearance that evening or his enlightening information. And there she went, thinking about him again.

Annoyed with herself, she fed Sam then started on dinner. Paul would like her spaghetti pie. There wasn't anyone she'd fixed it for who didn't, and it was one of her favorites. She ignored the phone when it rang while she was mixing the cooked pasta with butter, eggs, and parmesan. Her parents were away on a cruise, so it was likely Allie or Lily. While she enjoyed their friendship, they would want to bring up Slade, and she was trying hard not to dwell on whatever was going on between them.

She was closing the oven door when she heard someone drive up and got halfway to the door when Slade's loud voice followed his sharp rap.

"Nicole! Open up, or I'm coming in."

Flinging the door open with a scowl, she snapped, "What are you ranting about?"

"You didn't answer your phone," he stated in a relieved, much calmer tone than the strident worry she'd caught at first.

Moving back, she held the door open since it appeared he was coming in anyway. Nicole closed it with a sigh, betrayed again by that damn little skip in her pulse upon hearing him, the instant pleasure at seeing him again.

"I was busy. What did you want?"

Instead of answering, he sniffed, tossed

his lined denim coat on the sofa, and walked toward the kitchen, saying, "Smells like my timing is perfect. What are we having?"

"We?" She honestly couldn't think of anything else to say.

It was his turn to scowl at her, hands fisted on his hips, that darn sexy Stetson still tipped low, hiding his eyes. "Yes."

"You don't sound happy about it." About as pleased as she was, she imagined.

"I'm in the adjustment stage of our new relationship, same as you."

A few words and the man left her dumbfounded. "We're in a relationship?"

"Yes, and from watching my brothers this past year, eating together is apparently one of the things couples in a relationship do together. Where are the plates? I'll set the table."

She pointed to the cabinet behind him, delayed in questioning him further when Paul knocked on the back door. "That's Paul, my handyman. He arrived early and is getting a plate to take to the cottage. He didn't want to join me here. Respect that," she told Slade.

"Of course," he replied, setting his hat

on the counter.

*****

Nicole brushed by Slade, eyeing him as if she didn't believe him, before opening the back door. "Good timing. Come on in, and I'll take it out of the oven."

The new guy gazed at him with as much mistrust as Nicole, forcing Slade to throttle back his impatience. The instant, hair-trigger concern that sent him rushing over here when she didn't answer his call still hadn't eased all the way. Pretty soon, he would have no choice but to admit he'd already slipped from the milder L word to the deeper, more meaningful L word. He planned to take his brothers to task over not warning him about how love could sneak past, like without advance warning. It would have been nice to be prepared when it hit him in the face. For an ex-sniper, whose life had often depended on staying alert, that really rankled.

He held out his hand. "Slade Kincaid, the neighbor."

Paul nodded, his grasp strong enough to assure Slade he was up to the task of helping Nicole despite the recent rough years he'd suffered. "Lily's soon-to-be brother-in-law. Paul Westman. I don't mean to intrude…"

"You're not," Nicole cut in. "Are you sure you don't want to stay and eat with us?" She handed him a covered container big enough to hold several helpings.

"I'm sure, but thanks. I'd like to finish getting settled. I'll be up early to start work."

"Okay. I'll see you in the morning."

Slade spotted the plates as Nicole got out the container and set the table while she brought over a pan topped with melted Monterey Jack cheese. She set it down with a thump, the same way she took her seat, obviously still unhappy with this turn of events.

"I have water, beer, wine. Glasses above the sink. Help yourself. Spaghetti pie," she added, using a spatula to scoop a generous portion onto his plate.

"Looks and smells good. We'll have a glass of wine afterward."

She ignored that and started eating,

waiting to swallow before asking, "So, what did you want, when you called?"

"Nothing. See how you're doing, that sort of thing." He must be getting it bad when he found her scowl kind of cute.

"All this hassle because you just wanted to chitchat?"

Put that way, it made him irritable again. Before snapping in reply, like he was tempted to, he ate in silence, thinking of a better way to move forward instead of backward. Part of what he decided required baring more of himself, but he supposed that was necessary for a good relationship.

"Ever taken a walk on the wild side? Gone with or pursued any wild impulses?"

She thought a moment then said with decisiveness, "No."

"Ever want to?"

"No. I like things on an even keel, calm, easy. Why?"

Sucking it up, he admitted, "I have. As a military sniper. At first for the risk-taking adrenaline rush. Working for the greater good of saving lives proved a bonus."

"Until your last assignment."

"Yes, but even with the regret, I saved lives. As difficult it was, still can be, I've come to accept the boy as dead either way from the moment he was kidnapped. Now, it's your turn. Dare you to take that walk now."

Her lips quirked, a positive sign. "You want me to become a military sniper?"

"Funny girl. Lose the attitude. I'll do the same. See where this goes. Who knows, you may not go for my kink, and we'll call it quits."

"So, this is all about sex. I can do that, and try more of your kink."

She appeared happy to admit that, and Slade let her believe that's what he meant for now. It would help her lower her guard and leave her vulnerable to deeper feelings. And the fact he was psychoanalyzing proved how deeply invested he already was.

"More?" she inquired as he shoveled in the last bite.

"Sure. In case you can't tell, it was damn good."

Nicole handed him the spatula. "Thanks. Help yourself while I get the wine."

They ate seconds and drank wine, talking

about the renovations and her plans to foster. He hadn't thought to bring Chase until Sam kept giving him a look that said *where is he*? Slade figured he had pushed Nicole enough by the time they cleared the dishes and he picked up his hat.

"We usually go to Ina's for dinner midweek. I'll walk over early through the woods and show you the way to my place and then we'll leave from there."

She followed him to the door, not attempting to prolong his stay he noticed. "Is that your way of asking me to dinner?"

"Nope. Telling in case you've changed your mind already." He kissed her, hard and fast. The sex would wait until this weekend so as not to distract from either of their schedules. He still had to confront Evan Saturday morning when he was next scheduled to work, and preferred giving her his full concentration after he settled that disturbing matter. "Thanks for dinner."

Slade brought Chase with him Wednesday afternoon when he returned to Nicole's, taking the forest trail. Enough daylight remained to guide them back to his place with both dogs where they'd leave them while at dinner. He wanted Nicole and Sam to become familiar with the shortcut. As he and Chase emerged from the woods, they caught the tail end of Jim's work crew leaving and, from the looks of things, they would finish the kennels on schedule, by the weekend.

She opened the back door before he reached it, still shrugging on a single-breasted knee-length coat the color of oatmeal. Her short, dark hair swung around her chin as she closed it behind her and then gazed up at him with her bright-blue eyes clear for a nice change. "Ready?" It took work to tamp down his readiness for more than a simple dinner with family, like hauling her back inside and bending her over the kitchen table.

"I'm hungry, if that counts." She smiled, her eyes sliding to the dogs tussling with exuberant playfulness. "They sure like each other."

He clasped her hand and started across the yard. "Chase hasn't been around other dogs much, only my mother's. I keep him busy working with me, which he loves. The trail is easy to follow, but not so much at night."

"Oh, wow, it's so different in here," she said, walking through the trees alongside him. Do I hear water?"

"A creek, right around this curve." Even in the waning light, he could see the pleasure suffusing her face when they reached the bridge.

"This is so nice, and close enough to enjoy more at a warmer time. Sam! Damn it," she swore when the dogs chose to splash through the water instead of crossing the bridge with them. "Now I'll have to get a towel from you and dry him before we go."

"Relax. They'll shake most of it off and run the rest of the way. See? Sam's right on Chase's heels, and they'll beat us back."

"I'm used to protecting him. He was a malnourished stray, and it took Tony and I months to get him healthy and comfortable with us."

That was the first time Nicole had brought up her ex without remorse coloring her tone. Another positive indication in favor of this working. Now, if he could get past the shock of finding himself in this position and weather his brothers' ribbing without clocking them, he could sit back and enjoy the ride.

"You've done an admirable job." They reached the end of the trail with deepening dusk and drop in temperature. "And here we are."

*****

Nicole guessed Brett convinced Allie to refrain from saying anything about her and Slade arriving at Ina's together. That helped make dinner more enjoyable yet left her wondering what he'd told his family, if anything. She was still hesitant to believe this thing between them was anything more than mutual sexual interest. After mistaking the friendly attraction she'd felt toward Tony for the onset of something deeper developing, she remained cautious. However, continuing with the sex she could do with no problem.

"How nice to see this table filled with the Kincaids," Ina said, carrying over half of their orders with the waitress balancing the other half. "I was in the back when you got here." Her gaze went from Slade to Nicole, and she smiled with approval.

"It was this herb cheese soup that brought me in," she quipped lightly, taking in the large bowl of creamy soup thick with cod and broccoli and the generous slice of homemade bread.

"New recipe." Ina set a plate in front of Slade and one for Lily. "Save room for pie."

"Don't I always?" Brett replied, taking his stack of ribs from the server.

"You and Allie, yes." She laughed. "Reed and Slade aren't as devoted as you two."

"We are," Reed protested. "It's not my fault I can't resist seconds."

Lily nudged him with a teasing grin. "At home, he doesn't stop at seconds. Put me down for a slice of cherry, Ina."

That's a hunger pain, not a pang of longing for inclusion, Nicole insisted when her abdomen cramped listening to the banter. Since moving here, she'd missed her parents and friends on occasion, but overall was happy with her decision. More so now seeing the progress and envisioning Tony's approval of how she was spending his money. They had talked often about fostering, their busy schedules forcing them to put it off until she established herself as a graphic artist. She'd reached that goal when she'd snagged the contracts she had been in the process of fulfilling before leaving Chicago.

The work was fun, as she'd hoped, and between the new friendships and end to her long celibacy, her life here would have fulfilled a wish list if she'd had one. Other than her work, she owed the rest to Slade. She glanced at him as they ate, her heart executing that funny flip that started shortly after the night they'd gone upstairs at Casey's. It meant nothing, of course, just a reactive response to the sexuality he oozed in spades, so she put it out of her mind.

"Lily and I have an appointment with the caterer Friday afternoon, so we'll see you at Casey's," Reed stated as they all finished and prepared to leave.

"We'll get there early. I'm working with Jordon." Slade stood, picking up the check then taking Nicole's hand.

It took getting used to again, this couple thing. Nicole hadn't planned on going to Casey's both Friday and Saturday and clamped shut on pointing out his assumption since she'd agreed to give it a try. Instead, she tried to disregard the tingles from the slight abrasion of his calloused, rough skin and failed. Even his slightest touch was too potent to ignore.

"I'm so glad Paul is with you and the job is going well," Lily told Nicole when they stepped to the side so the guys could pay at the counter.

"We're getting along good, and he seems to enjoy physical labor. Jim, my contractor, is also happy to have his help."

Allie and Brett turned to leave. "See you this weekend," she said with a wave.

"A little late, but we'll be there," Lily replied.

Nicole lifted her hand, still adjusting to the commitment she'd made to Slade and this whole dating thing again. She made herself cough up some more of that adjustment when they arrived back at her place and her phone beeped with an incoming text. A quick peek revealed Natalie's name, as she'd suspected, and she pressed delete.

Ever astute, he shut off the truck, turned her way, and asked, "Is someone harassing you, Nicole?"

She didn't want to involve him in her ongoing saga with Natalie but saw no way around it now. "Tony's twin sister can't get past her grief and blames me. She's harmless, the texts idle threats she doesn't mean."

"Don't take any threats lightly. You should report them." Slade opened his door. "Do you mind if I see the progress Jim is making?"

"No, go ahead. I have to get back to work."

Flashing her a grin, he asked, "You're not ready to show me your illustrations, are you?"

She was trying not to think about how his rare smile gave her tingles when she answered. "Not yet. When this book is done, maybe. Thanks for lunch." She never shared her drawings until she finished a story. In her mind, they looked better coming together to tell the tale without reading the words, depicting what made a child happy with reading the book.

"I'll hold you to that. Does six on Friday work for you? We can get something to eat first."

"Sure," Nicole replied, acting like it was nothing more than a date, when the thrill of going upstairs with Slade again at Casey's shot through her. Maybe one more night would get her over this lust-induced infatuation she kept swearing she wasn't ready for.

Chapter Twelve

By Friday afternoon, Nicole felt pretty darn good watching Jim load up to leave. Eyeing the new outdoor portion of the kennels with Paul, she couldn't be more pleased with the contractor's work. "What do you think?" she asked her handyman who was also proving to work out as well as Jim's crew.

"I think you're looking as forward to working on the dogs waiting for you as I am to learn how to rehabilitate poorly treated ones," he replied.

"You can ride in with me tomorrow to pick up the three the shelter is in need of finding space and positive training for. They've agreed to send the potential adopters out here and let me make that decision when I deem the dogs are ready, which I appreciate.

I'd like that extra assurance of knowing they're going to good homes. Let's go inside."

They entered the barn, which looked completely different than two weeks ago. Sheetrock now covered the walls, behind which she knew lay enough insulation to keep the large space warm. Running the electric heat out here would keep it warm during the frigid winter months and by adding cross ventilation with more windows and large ceiling fans, the shelter would stay comfortable during milder weather. The five kennels with dog doors leading to the outdoor space were each spacious enough for two large dogs to have plenty of room to roam around when not playing in the enclosed yard. New concrete floor covered the rest of the barn, storage along the opposite wall for supplies and food, and enough space in between to work with the dogs indoors if the temperature wasn't conducive outdoors.

"See anything we missed or you'd like added?" Jim asked, joining them.

"I can't think of a thing, Jim. Thank you so much," she said, signing the form he handed her. "It looks better than I imagined.

You even left space to add a few more kennels. I never thought of that."

"Much easier to do that now, leaving little more than putting up the pens and adding a dog door if you ever need them. Appreciate the work."

"Put me down for referrals. That's the least I can do for you."

Nicole handed the form back and they walked out together. With business completed for now, she could concentrate on getting ready for Slade and ending the plaguing scenarios running through her head the past few days about what he had planned. The sooner she could get over this constant need tormenting her since meeting him, the sooner she could give her full concentration to starting over with the dream she'd shared with Tony. With luck, fulfilling that dream for both of them would lay to rest the last of her lingering guilt over his death.

"Will do. Have a good weekend."

Paul nodded to them. "Now that you've finished the last touches on the cottage also, and if you don't need me, Lily has collected a few items I'd like to pick up and do a few things for the shelter while I'm there."

"You go ahead. I have plans with Slade shortly." He'd worked as hard as Jim's guys this week and deserved a break.

They said goodbye to Jim and his crew then Paul turned to her, appearing awkward as he stated, "I'll be back tonight so you won't be alone out here, you know, in case Slade doesn't stay."

She grinned, appreciating his thoughtfulness and concern despite his obvious discomfort with referencing her and Slade's relationship. He really was a nice guy trying to turn his life around. "Honestly, I have no idea, so thanks, but still, don't rush on my account. We'll be out awhile. Talk to you tomorrow."

Calling Sam, they went inside where she decided it was too damn cold for anything sexy that left part of her bare, like legs, arms, or too much neckline. Besides, Slade seemed to have no trouble getting turned on when she dressed in her usual jeans and plain tops, which admittedly was an ego-boosting turn-on for her. While it was still light out, she opened the door for Sam to do his business and run around a little more before Slade showed up.

Not five minutes later, his frantic barking sent her dashing outside again to check on him. Shivering, she scanned the yard and went rigid spotting him chasing what looked like the tail end of a coyote into the woods. Panicking, she ran after him, calling, "Sam, no!" At least the dense trees blocked the wind, making following the trail a little warmer since her dog wasn't answering her calls. From his faint barking, he was already way ahead of her and running in the opposite direction of the creek crossing to reach Slade's house. She was too scared for Sam, though, to worry about Slade's reaction if they didn't make it back before he arrived.

*****

Sitting up on this higher slope for hours waiting for an opportune time to take Wells out has put me in a foul mood, more than ready to get this over with and out of here. Waiting until I was sure the workers and the new guy weren't returning would have worked once she'd let the dog out. I planned to do the deed when she came out to call him in, saving me from sneaking up to the house and getting up close and personal to kill her. She'd caught me unaware when she'd run pell-mell into the woods after the mutt, but as I'm tracking her, I think this will work out even better. Her death will be blamed on a careless hunter and I'll be long gone, back in Chicago.

Perfect.

*****

After this, Nicole swore Sam would lose his running-free privileges. It would be the fenced yard from now on. A good ten minutes later, she found him sniffing for a clue where to go next, both of them out of breath. "Come, now," she ordered, using her no-nonsense voice. He started to slink over when a shot rang out, barely missing him and startling them both into full-fledged panic.

"*Shit.*" Crouching down, praying it was

just a stray bullet from a hunter, she fought off fear-induced hysteria and grabbed Sam's collar. Through the trees, she could detect a small rise and crept in that direction, staying low. They reached it as another gunshot rent the air, sending birds scattering and the two of them running for cover. She was unable to tell how far away the shots were coming from, or even which direction, but planned to stay crouched behind the relative safety of the tree-covered ridge until she was in jeopardy of freezing to death.

*****

Fuck! Now I'll have to move in closer and I didn't want to get that far from the car. No help for it though. After taking the chance on such a long-distance shot and missing, I'm out of options. I've blown any possibility of returning for a third opportunity. It's now or never.

*****

Slade paused in the drive, the echo of a gunshot in the woods giving him concern. Hunters rarely strayed this close to ranches and with Nicole not knowing how near that shot resonated from, she could be outside with Sam. Grabbing his rifle out of the truck, he hurried through the wooded path to her place, something telling him all was not right. That sixth sense proved correct when the second shot rang much louder as he reached the center of the trail.

He scanned her yard as he ran toward the house, not seeing her or Paul outside. After pounding on the door and not hearing either her or Sam, he let himself inside, the unlocked door and empty house giving him more cause for alarm. Returning outside, he breathed a sigh of relief seeing Paul drive up, hoping he would know where Nicole was.

"What's wrong?" Paul asked as soon as he got out and saw Slade.

"I can't find Nicole, or Sam. Do you…" Another report rent the air, drawing a curse.

"Crap, I bet she took off after the dog. Into the woods." Now the handyman looked as worried as Slade felt. "I was headed into town but was uneasy about leaving her before you got here and turned around."

"Which direction should I go?"

Pointing, he said, "Pretty sure that way. I'll come with you."

"No, stay here in case she returns," he tossed out as he took off. "Call the cops and my brothers." He didn't have a spare moment to pull out his phone and make the calls himself right now. Finding Nicole before she got hit by the idiot hunter who appeared to lack a lick of hunting sense was his number one goal.

The dense woods turned eerily silent as he moved with speed while searching for clues as to where Nicole or Sam had gone. From years of playing in this particular forested area, he knew every inch of it by heart. This stretch of trees wasn't as wide as long. He came into view of the short ridge and took the risk of calling out for her.

"Nicole!"

"Here, Slade!"

Her dark head popped up over the hill when a bullet slammed into the ground inches from her face. "Get down!" he shouted, realizing whoever that was, he was gunning for her. Lifting his rifle, he shot in the direction of the hunter as he ran to Nicole, his arm stinging with a minor flesh wound in the process.

"You're bleeding," she gasped, grabbing his arm when he hunkered down next to them.

Sam lay cowering beside her, the poor dog shaking like a leaf. "I'm fine. Listen. There's an old hunting cabin not two, three hundred yards that way." He nodded toward the trees on his left. "Grab Sam and haul ass toward it as soon as I start firing. Got it?"

"What about you?" Her voice shook, but her eyes held an angry, determined glint he was glad to see.

"I'll be right behind you. Don't argue. Just go. Ready?"

At her nod, he stood and fired, walking backward the few feet into the safety of the woods again before spinning around and rushing inside the old one-room cabin. He slammed the door then drew a deep breath and dragged the worn armchair in front of it.

"What's going on, Slade?" She sat on

a rickety chair at the dust-covered table, stroking Sam, her face tense, her blue eyes stormy.

"That's what *you're* going to tell *me*. I'm guessing those texts weren't as harmless as you thought."

"You think Natalie's trying to *kill* me?" She shook her head, still refusing to consider that possibility. "No, I can't believe she is that unhinged. Mad and grieving, yes, but not deranged. It must be a hunter chasing something we haven't seen."

Slade leaned against the wall by the one window, reverting to sniper-mode watchfulness while he tried to stay patient with Nicole. "Set aside the woman she was before Tony's death, go through those texts with an open mind to the possibility, and give me more info on this family. Anything you can tell me. You never know what small tidbit will help in a situation like this."

"Can't you call the cops and wait for them?"

"Paul is doing that, and getting hold of my brothers, who are a lot closer. He returned right after I got to your place. Help is coming, but I don't want *anyone* hurt here, not if I can help it."

*****

Brett swore as he read a text from Nicole's new handyman. He replied, telling Paul they were on their way, and then strode from the stable toward the corral where Reed was talking to Keith and Evan in Slade's place, urgency in every step he took and his tone when he addressed his brother.

"We have to go now. Slade and Nicole are in trouble."

For some reason, Evan's face paled, and he joined Reed in withdrawing his rifle from the scabbard on his mount. "I'm going with you."

"Fuck that. You're enough trouble around here. This is our brother we're talking about," Reed snapped.

"He's my brother too," Evan announced, shocking both Reed and Brett into a moment of stunned silence.

Brett recovered first, stating, "Explain

on the way. Keith, hang until you hear from one of us."

"Yes, sir." Worry colored the young man's voice. "Be careful."

The three of them got into Brett's truck, Evan in the rear. Brett sped toward the wooded area Paul mentioned, knowing where he was talking about, just not their exact location within those trees. "Explain," he ordered Evan as they bounced across the rougher terrain of the fields.

"Yeah, let's hear this cock-and-bull story."

"Reed." Brett used his stern, older-brother voice to calm down Reed who appeared closed-minded to Evan's declaration.

"Jesus, you grew up with the old man's public womanizing and doubt he could sire another kid?" he answered with bitterness. "Well, guess what? It's true, according to my mom. I'm the result of their brief fling, which I learned about as a high school graduation gift. All those years of watching my mom struggle to make ends meet, while dear old Dad could afford to help us."

"That's why you took the job, to get even through the malicious pranks?" Brett inquired, feeling bad for the kid. His story would be simple enough to check out, which Evan must realize. That alone made it easier for him to believe, but when he added Casey's reputation into it, there was no plausible reason to discount Evan's claim outright. Reed's shrug as he looked his way signaled he agreed with Brett's thoughts.

Evan blew out a breath and turned his face aside, toward the window. "Yes. I'm sorry, I never wanted to see any of you hurt or the blame to land on anyone else."

"Let's finish this later and concentrate now on finding Slade and Nicole," Reed suggested when Brett parked as close as he could get to the area Paul had mentioned.

"Agreed. Stay behind us, Evan, and keep your gun ready. We don't know what's..." A shot echoed from the trees, prompting them to move faster. "This way. Move fast but carefully."

*****

Sam lay down, finally relaxing, and Nicole stood to pace while flipping through her texts. She still couldn't wrap her head around Slade's assumption about Natalie. Whenever they spent time with Tony's sister, she would spout nonsense or outrage over something or someone. She swore that girl wasn't happy unless she was on a tirade. Tony had certainly never taken her seriously. Regardless, she would do Slade's bidding just to make *him* happy.

She paced back and forth, opening the texts she'd ignored and reading them while pausing to glance toward Slade, her gaze constantly dragged his way by an invisible magnet. Each time, her heart flipped and her pulse jumped. An odd place and situation for her to crave what he was so damn good at delivering, but since when did common sense rule her body? At a minimum, not since she'd met the rugged cowboy looking at her with sharp concern reflected in his silver eyes. She'd never imagined the impact or the pleasure of having a man's focus stay so attuned to her every word, gesture, and need whenever they were together, regardless of where. The reward of that intense fixation was an irresistible, unquestionable aphrodisiac, impossible to ignore or trivialize.

While coming to terms with the impact of Natalie's threatening texts that she'd ignored, another reality slowly unfurled deep inside her. Not since first meeting Tony had she been so drawn to a man, and their relationship had been the closest she'd ever gotten to falling in love. She always figured she would know when the feeling was right, when the big L bit her on the ass. It would come at her out of the blue, likely an unexpected time or place, from someone she'd never imagined herself falling for. That's what had deceived her about Tony in the beginning yet never panned out. With a sigh of disgust, she thought the real deal would drive her nuts, but she would hunger for him regardless. He would be there for her even though she didn't want...

Nicole swung to face Slade. *"Ahh, shit."*

"What's bugging you now?" he asked, his tone testy as he divided his attention between watching for the shooter and her.

"You," she snapped. Admitting she was

gone over the guy was a hard pill to swallow.

He tossed her a peevish glare. "Me? What did I do other than prove I'm right about those texts you've been studying?"

"Oh, it's not these." She held up the phone, returning his hard look. "You just had to worm your way into my life, didn't you, with the whole sexy cowboy swagger and friendly assistance. Then, as if the hot sex wasn't enough of a capper, you got all protective, riding to my rescue, even getting hurt in the process. What woman in her right mind could resist falling in love with you? Just answer me that, damn it." She fumed, fisting her hands on her hips when his lips quirked. "Oh, don't you dare smile now, Slade Kincaid."

A shot rang out, hitting right next to the window. "Get down! We'll discuss your epiphany later."

She didn't argue, dashing to crouch behind the worn sofa, Sam joining her without being called as Slade returned fire. More shots ricocheted, these coming from the front of the cabin, whizzing by in the direction of the shooter. Breathing a sigh of relief, she realized help had arrived and, with luck, would aid in ending this standoff quickly.

It didn't take long. There were more shots exchanged between Slade and whoever had arrived to help and the shooter. Nicole still grappled with the lengths Natalie had gone to, to take out her grief and revenge on her. All it accomplished was to enlighten the fact she wasn't responsible for Tony's diagnosis or the pain that had ultimately resulted in his death. She could now admit the sequence of events that left her scarred and killing him was unfortunate but not her fault.

Despite the battle waging outside this small cabin, a huge weight lifted from her conscience. The loud, rapid reports ended on that thought, the silence almost eerie after the constant noise reverberating for the past five to ten minutes. Shouts came from several directions seconds before Brett and Reed called Slade's name then rushed inside.

"We're fine," Slade hurried to reassure his brothers, rising and holding his hand out for her without taking his eyes off his siblings and Evan who followed them inside.

That simple gesture drew her out from behind the sofa, her heart turning over, an onslaught of emotion overwhelming her all at once. She fought to get herself under control, needing time and space to assimilate all the repercussions of the evening. That need increased as they left the cabin and saw law enforcement officials leading a handcuffed Michael Renaldi toward them.

"Michael, you?" Nicole squeaked in disbelief.

She stood there in stunned disbelief. Of the three Renaldi siblings, Michael was the last one she would consider doing such a thing. The oldest family member always seemed so in command of himself, the family business, and his siblings, in that order.

"I wasn't about to let Natalie destroy her future or our name. I was protecting her against herself."

Slade stepped forward, brushing off Brett's attempt to hold him back. "That's your excuse for attempting to kill Nicole, and me? The only thing protecting you now from my wrath is those handcuffs."

It's a part of him, of who he is, Nicole

mused, shaking her head at Slade's seemingly endless capacity to safeguard the oppressed.

Reed moved between Slade and the county sheriffs holding Renaldi. "Moore, Jenkins, good to see you. Thanks for responding so fast. Where are you taking him?"

"Into Casper. They'll book him at the main precinct. Ma'am," the one responding addressed Nicole. "You'll have to give a statement, both of you, sometime tomorrow will be soon enough."

"Sure," Nicole answered, still in a daze from the revelations of the past hour, the least of which were her deep feelings for the annoying neighbor, sex-on-a-stick rancher, and chivalrous man whom she never thought of as her type. Love had hit her so fast, so hard, like an unexpected punch to the face, that she'd gone into instant, angry defense mode. It would be a while before she could come to terms with just that, let alone Tony's family's attempt at retribution.

"Thanks, guys," Brett said as the officers led Renaldi to their vehicle.

"No problem." The cop yanked on

Renaldi's arm as he spouted about his slew of lawyers. "Shut up," he told him.

Slade hugged Nicole to his side with one arm and reached down to pet Sam with the other while addressing his brothers. "Thanks. Mind giving us a ride back?"

"Come on. Let's get out of here. I hope that's a flesh wound." Brett nodded toward his arm, shouldered his rifle, and pivoted, Reed following him.

"It is. I'll take care of it."

Nicole leaned into Slade's warmth, shivering against the cold air as they walked around the old cabin and back through the woods to where they'd left their truck. Slade paused when they saw one of his hired hands at the truck.

"Evan, what are you doing here?"

He didn't sound happy about seeing the young man he regarded with suspicion.

"It can wait," Reed stated before Evan could reply. "First things first. Your girl is freezing, your arm needs tending, and this poor guy is still scared." He reached down to pet Sam, but he wouldn't budge from Nicole's side.

"You're right. Sorry, Nicole."

As he lifted her onto the back seat, she noticed he didn't refute his brother calling her his girl. That was enough to warm her. Either that or her brain wasn't functioning yet after the trauma-laden evening. Nicole didn't want to second-guess anything anymore though. Everything could wait until she put the past and the Renaldis to rest. Then she could think clearly about the present, and maybe the future.

Chapter Thirteen

Slade spent the return trip from the cabin, juggling his need to speak with Evan and his desire to indulge in a heart-to-heart candid talk with Nicole. She had rendered him speechless with her less-than-enthusiastic declaration of love, although, he believed he hid his surprise well. Suspecting her feelings were running as deep as his own wasn't the same as hearing her announce it. One of his rare cases of amusement had tickled his throat at her disgruntled attitude, then again, he could easily recall his own reluctance to accept he'd gone down the same path he'd been teasing his brothers about these many months.

Nicole's head rested against his shoulder, Sam's head on her thigh, with Evan seated next to her. He could see exhaustion on her pale face and around her closed eyes, feel it in her slumped body. Evan kept his face averted and didn't talk. Slade held her hand and decided to let her rest and assimilate her thoughts while he returned home to speak with his brothers and Evan. She was made of sturdy stuff, his girl, and would be fine until he returned to her place in a few hours. Tomorrow they would go into Casper together and give their statements. Knowing her, Nicole would want to confront Michael Renaldi, would need to get answers before she could move past what had happened between her and Tony. God knew he'd faced his conscience more than once before allowing his brothers in and finally coming to terms with his actions.

"Drop Nicole off first, Brett," he said even though he still shuddered from how close to harm, or worse, she'd come. "Reed, is there any way to find out where the other two Renaldi siblings are?" It just occurred to him they too might be nearby and in on the eldest's actions.

"Already on it and waiting for an answer."

Nicole stirred and lifted her head.

"You think they might have come here with Michael? I can't see the three of them bonding together to commit such an act."

"Yet, you sounded surprised when you saw your shooter," Brett pointed out.

"I was, still am. Tony's twin was the one sending me threatening texts ever since he died. And Doug was angry when I rebuffed his attempt to get me to sleep with him." Her soft lips curled in a sneer. "The guy's a man whore and first-class jerk."

This time, Slade let his humor show in a smile. Her fierce tone proved the evening's events had put a dent in her, but she was far from damaged. "Wish I had seen that put-down," he murmured in her ear.

Instead of replying to that comment, she sat up straight as Brett pulled into her drive. "How'd we get back so fast?"

"You zoned out for a while. It takes longer driving around the woods than walking through them." He opened his door when Brett parked, addressing his brother. "Give me a minute, will you? We can talk at my place."

Swiveling around from the driver's seat,

he said, "No problem. Take care, Nicole. I'll keep Allie from rushing over, at least until you give your statement tomorrow."

Reed agreed. "Lily will wait also."

Evan didn't speak until Nicole slid out. "I'm glad you're okay, both of you."

"Thanks to all of you. Good night."

She appeared relieved he wasn't staying then pleased when he stated at the door, "I'll return in a little while. There's Paul." He nodded to the handyman standing outside his cottage, his hand lifted in acknowledgement of their safe return.

"He's one of the few things I did right since moving here. Go. I'm fine."

He gave her a quick kiss, itching to stay regardless of her obvious need for the chance to regroup. Returning to the truck, he wished for once, life would go easy. Since that wasn't likely to happen, he addressed the next pressing issue sitting next to him as they headed back to the ranch, pinning Evan with a direct look and comment.

"Tell me why. I already figured out you're the one behind the vandalism these past months."

"Yes, tell him, Evan," Reed drawled with underlying humor.

Slade cut his gaze to Reed, not appreciating his amusement. "All those pranks were not funny."

"Don't get mad at anyone except me." Guilt suffused the younger man's face, but he didn't shift away from Slade's pointed stare again. "Casey Kincaid was my father too. My mother broke the news to me when I graduated high school. She never told him about me because she wanted nothing more to do with him after he dumped her. I was pissed, missing out on having brothers and yes, sharing in the Kincaid ranch." His chin went up in defiance at odds with the regret shimmering in his green eyes, eyes the same shade as their father's.

"His claim is easy to verify through a simple DNA test. Reed and I figured he was telling the truth. That, and we can now see Kincaid written all over him, in looks and attitude," Brett said.

"Your behavior, however, was not that of a Kincaid." Slade had no problem believing their dad had sired another kid, and could drum up compassion for the teenager dealing with that news. Forgiving him outright for his retaliation was another matter. "You did a lot of damage, and I'm not talking about materialistic harm we can afford to replace. Relationships, if you want them, will have to be repaired, which requires effort from you money can't buy."

Evan looked at each of them then asked him, "Are you willing to let me try?"

What the hell, he mused. At his age, he never thought he would have another sibling or want to settle down in a committed relationship. But he'd quit trying to understand human nature when he couldn't stay away from the unwelcoming neighbor.

Brett pulled into Slade's driveway then swiveled to look at Evan. "I am, but I still want DNA confirmation before we discuss a four-way partnership in the ranch. I agree with Slade. You have to earn our trust before you can reap the rewards of our father's hard work and legacy."

The outdoor lights came on automatically, shedding illumination in the dark. Opening the door, Slade told Evan, "Go home, come clean with your friends, and return to work tomorrow." The rest was up to the kid. "Thanks again. I'm going to get Chase and return to Nicole's. See you tomorrow."

He went inside and fed Chase, cleaned up the bullet graze on his arm and wrapped it, then made a quick sandwich. After tossing a few things in an overnight bag, he couldn't wait another minute to drive back to Nicole. The drastic change in plans from going to Casey's to finding himself aiming a gun at a person again had left him drained, even though the hour wasn't that late. He knew she was as emotionally and physically exhausted as he, and planned to do nothing more than relax and just be with her, without pressure or angst between them.

Nicole's light above the front door was on, and he rapped twice then entered to see her taking a seat at the table across from Paul. "We're having meat loaf. Did you eat?"

"I grabbed a sandwich." Making himself at home, he hung up his jacket and hat and walked around the wrestling dogs to join them. "There's always room for meat loaf though. Paul, thank you for getting hold of everyone."

"Nicole filled me in and it sounds like I had the easy task," he answered, taking the spatula from her to serve himself.

"Over and done with. Talk about something else," she insisted.

Slade recognized the glint in her eyes and the determination stamped on her face. Wasn't that gumption one of the things he admired first about her? She might get frayed around the edges, yet she continued to maintain that admirable trait of holding her own following a strenuous ordeal.

"Okay. It looks like you're ready to start fostering. Why don't we stop at the shelter tomorrow after giving our statements and bring back the dogs they have for you to foster?"

Her eyes lit up at that suggestion, and they spoke of her plans and what Paul's role would be going forward. It didn't surprise him when she expressed a desire to take in neglected horses once she learned more about the care they required. The traumatic episode that ended with Tony's death at her hands hadn't deterred her from her ambitious career goals of illustrating children's books while continuing to help ill-treated animals in some capacity.

"I can help you with that," he offered as they cleared the table. "Along with veterinary care, you'll need regular hoof maintenance from a farrier and dental checkups."

"I went with my wife to our kids' riding lessons once."

Nicole closed the dishwasher, glancing at Paul with compassion. "That sounds like a good memory."

"It is. I'll turn in now, and do the chores while you're gone tomorrow. Thank you for dinner." He grinned at Slade. "Don't worry. I don't plan on intruding on you two every night."

"You're welcome any time I'm here, Paul."

Lily had done right by this man, he mused, thinking his brother had also made an excellent choice when he'd pursued his fiancée. After Paul left and they let the dogs out for a few minutes, Slade drew Nicole onto his lap on the sofa and picked up the remote control for the television.

"Relax. I want to say one thing and then we'll find a movie and sit quietly before turning in."

The tenseness went out of her muscles, and she leaned against him. "Okay. What do you want to say?"

"Only that I reciprocate your feelings."

*****

Nicole sank against Slade's chest, relieved to hear him say that. Now she could allow herself to enjoy his comforting embrace when he wrapped his arms around her, appreciating his keen insight for once. The harrowing moments cringing behind the ridge followed by Slade's rescue had left her body and mind drained.

She let him pick the movie, *The Lincoln Lawyer*, which she'd never seen. The plot kept her engrossed and awake until the end. The silence between them seemed natural, and it wasn't until the credits started rolling and he nudged her up that she broke it.

"Good movie. Thanks. I work on my

illustrations in the evenings and rarely sit down to watch a show." He rose, towering over her, and she resisted the urge to lean on him again. "You brought a bag, so I'm assuming you're staying the night?"

"It's been a while since I saw it, and yes, I'm staying the night." Taking her hand, he tugged her toward the hall. "Which room?"

"Second on the right. Slade…"

"We're going to get undressed and go to sleep, Nicole," he interrupted, entering her bedroom where he faced her. "That's all, tonight. We love each other. How that happened, or why, doesn't seem to matter. Any other issues we'll deal with later. And I'm beat."

Nicole relaxed and pulled off her top. Of course he would know what she wanted and needed. That might be one of the issues that would take some getting used to. "Bathroom's across the hall. Me first."

She was in bed when he finished and turned off the light. The mattress dipped with his weight, and she rolled against his warm naked strength with a sigh, his rough fingers tracing her scars the last thing that registered before sleep took over.

*****

Excitement hummed inside Nicole as Slade parked at Casey's. Tonight marked her third visit to the Kincaid's playroom above the club, and her first play party. She didn't have a clue what he had planned, which was nothing new. That was one of only a few things that hadn't changed since the day he'd emerged from the woods separating their places, unfazed by her attitude toward his unexpected, unwelcome visit. She wouldn't tell him, but since acknowledging her feelings, she'd grown to like the way he would just swoop in and take over when she needed him to. Her recent move into his house, however, proved she wasn't about to let him coddle her every time she hit a snag. Earlier today, they'd both agreed they would work on remaining patient while adjusting to the changes necessary for any relationship to survive.

That meant compromise, something he

was better at than she.

"Nervous?" he asked.

"No, not really. You've said I met your friends who will be here."

"Be sure and let me know if you're uneasy seeing any of them wielding a flogger or strapped naked on an apparatus. I'll help you down."

She waited for him to come around to open the door even though she could easily hop off the high seat. Not since that eye-opening day two months ago had she passed up an opportunity to get close to him. Life was too short to deny even the smallest uplifting gift. Their coats didn't prevent his warmth from enveloping her as she fell against him, her hands braced on his shoulders, and she hoped that never changed.

Following him up the stairs, Nicole considered all the changes she now counted as blessings. With Michael busy fighting for the best deal possible, which would include significant jail time the DA promised, and his siblings suddenly finding their hands full hanging onto the family business and fortunes, she was free of them. The decision to foster had gone so well, she couldn't imagine doing anything else from now on. With Paul's invaluable help and friendship, they'd rehomed three dogs already and were caring for six more, along with two miniature horses she might adopt herself. Could she help it if she was a sucker for those cute, small equines? They'd moved Paul into the house, and now she used the cottage for an office, sometimes taking advantage of the alone time to work on her illustrations without Slade distracting her.

Talk about distractions, she thought, entering the upstairs room and seeing it occupied with others for the first time. Slade brought her back here two days after they'd given their depositions instead of that night and introduced her to bondage on a padded bench. She'd succumbed to his control with the same benefits as when he'd pinned her hands and hips on the sofa now occupied by another couple, her reward the freedom to simply let go without reservation or thought. Regardless of the audience, she ached for that same outcome tonight as they socialized.

"Incoming," Slade murmured, helping

her off with her coat.

Before she could ask what he meant, Allie was there, beaming and twirling, the satin babydoll nightie she wore skimming her upper thighs and clinging to her nipples. "What do you think? Brett surprised me with it."

"It's you," Nicole replied, wishing she owned something sexier than jeans and the fitted knit top she tucked into them. Taking a quick scan of the other women confirmed her overdressed state, and she cringed inside. "It appears I didn't dress suitably."

"You're fine. I just wanted to show it off and tell you how glad I am you're here. We'll talk later." She skipped away with a spin and finger wave, revealing the thong that left her buttocks bare.

"I agree, you look fine," Slade reassured her, brushing a hand over her backside. "Let me hang these up then we'll get a drink."

Despite the provocative scenes taking place, her gaze followed him as he hung their coats and his hat on a wall rack. She'd quit trying to understand how her annoyance had switched to such intense feelings in so short a time, having discovered it was easier and more enjoyable to go with the flow.

"Nicole, come join me." Lily motioned to the chair beside hers as they neared where she sat close to the burning fireplace. "Do you mind, Slade?"

"Not at all. What do you want from the bar?" he asked Nicole.

"An Amaretto sour," she replied, her usual light choice when she wanted to keep a clear head.

He nodded and glanced toward Lily. "Lily?"

"I'm good." She lifted the half-full glass sitting on the corner table beside her.

Reed strolled behind her chair and rested his hands on her shoulders. "More than good. Glad you two could make it."

Nicole only caught bits and pieces of the brothers' brief talk, unable to drag her attention off the casual way Reed slid his hands downward, into the low-scooped neckline of Lily's silk, thin-strapped tee. His fingers toyed with her bare nipples, his gaze remaining steady on her and Slade, Lily's acceptance of his public fondling and the pleasure etched on her pink face, heightening Nicole's constant craving for Slade's touch. There was nothing new with that though. Since that first night in this room, hooking up for sex had been easy, the decision made by her body without consulting her head. She could pay better attention once Slade walked away to get their drinks, and Reed traded places with Lily to settle her on his lap.

As if reading her mind, Reed said, "Don't dwell on anything except enjoying yourself tonight, Nicole. I'm sure Slade mentioned something of the sort."

"He did, but it's difficult not to," she answered with honesty.

Lily laughed. "Been there, agree with that. My advice, fixate on Slade."

"Again, difficult not to," she answered with a wry grin.

Slade returned, handing her the glass. "Not to what?"

"Keep her attention on you and not, say, Bianca strapped on the swing over there." Reed gestured toward a corner where the lighting was dimmer.

Naturally, her gaze swung in that

direction, her face turning hot encountering Casey's bartender's flexing buttocks as he drove between the woman's raised, spread thighs on a meshed contraption. The blatant position didn't seem to bother the woman, Nicole thought, not with their attention so fixated on each other. She sipped her drink, easing the dryness in her throat until Slade gripped her elbow, urging her to stand.

"Come with me."

A frisson of molten heat rushed to her head as she rose, downing a long swallow. "Where to?"

Instead of answering, he steered her toward the hall.

"See you later, Lily," she tossed over her shoulder, more than willing to follow him.

"Have fun."

Nicole questioned "fun" when he led her into the room with a raised table that looked too similar to what she lay on at her gynecologist for her peace of mind, and said one word.

"Strip."

"Uh, Slade?" She paused, yearning to get naked yet unsure about that much exposure tonight, then breathed easier as he closed the shades, blocking out viewers.

"Give me some credit, Nicole." He removed her clothes himself, his fingers skimming each bare exposure as he went. "You're lucky I waited as long as I did once I saw your expression when we came in."

I should have known. "My bad," she admitted, a shiver dancing down her spine as he lifted her onto the padded table, putting her nipples close to his mouth.

He gave each nub a slow tongue swipe, murmuring, "*Mmm*, what should I do about that?" Lifting his hands to her shoulders, he pressed her down then positioned her lower legs on the elevated side pads.

Nicole grabbed the side handles, damp and ready for whatever he planned, her arousal spiking when he retrieved a feather-tipped toy from a cabinet. "What's that?" On the other end of the short rod was a leather square.

"A mini spanker. You'll like it."

Slade drew a strap across her hips, leaving her lower body spread and immobile. Holding tighter to the handles, she braced for the impact of each end. "If you say so... *Oh!*" she exclaimed, the slow caress of the feather between her legs sending her arousal soaring. The abrupt sting from the snapper in the same spot snagged her breath as she strained to shift with the burn.

"I'm sure," he taunted, slipping two fingers inside her pussy.

Through the never-ending procession of tickle, slap strokes that followed, Nicole's focus never wavered from the man standing in front of her; not when the pleasure pain grew so intense, it threatened her sanity; not when Slade replaced the toy and his fingers with his cock; and not when her orgasm encompassed her entire body. *I should have known,* was her first thought when she came down from the euphoric high and realized she hadn't wasted a moment thinking about where they were or the people right outside of this room. Hadn't it been that way since she'd first clapped eyes on him?

"What's going through that head of yours?" Slade asked, pulling out of her still-clutching sheath with an indulgent grin.

"How glad I am you didn't let me run

you off."

"When I couldn't stay away, I finally believed what my brothers were telling me – when it's right, it's right."

Epilogue

Slade stood in a corner of the crowded hospital room, observing his family with amusement and love. His chest tightened as he gazed at his nephew cradled in Allie's arms where she lay on the bed, never imagining a new life could hold such meaning for him. No one but he knew today was the anniversary of the first time he'd shot a rifle to kill someone, saving an entire U.S. Army unit. The depth of his feelings no longer surprised him or required a period of adjustment, thanks mostly to his wife of one week. Marrying the cranky neighbor he'd first met had been the easiest, most natural decision to make, and he couldn't recall a better time. He looked at Brett who stood beside the bed, his green eyes reflecting a proud glow as he ran his knuckles down his wife's tired face. He'd stayed with her while she labored more than eight hours, Slade and the family arriving over an hour ago. He had never seen his oldest brother happier.

He took in Nicole's shoulder-length black hair and shining blue eyes when Allie handed her little Carson. Yeah, he could picture her with an infant of their own soon. Not yet, but they could start working on that after Lily delivered. His other sister-in-law sat next to Nicole and leaned forward to coo over the baby, Reed behind her still appearing thunderstruck over hearing he had fathered twins. Slade and Brett had gotten in a good laugh at his face yesterday when Lily called to tell him.

His mother joined him, her smile saying it all. "It's a good day, isn't it?"

"One of the best." Slinging an arm around her shoulders, he hugged her then kissed her cheek. "And so are you, in case I never mentioned that."

"It's always nice to get a compliment from one of my sons. You know, he may not have been a good husband or a very responsible father, but Casey tried, and you boys took notice."

"He should have done better, Mom, but you're right. We did everything possible not to turn out like Dad."

"And look how well all three of you have done." She hugged him back with a sigh then moved out of his embrace. "I'm proud of the way you've accepted Evan and included him in our lives. He's a good kid."

"Well, *now* he is." Evan had come a long way in earning their trust, the extra effort he continued to exert at the ranch garnering their respect. Slade cared for him, as did Brett and Reed, and he would have been here today if it weren't the first day of the fall semester.

"Thanks to you boys. Now, we'd best get you to the airport. That small island resort you and Nicole booked sounds wonderful."

It did, as superb as their future, Slade thought, striding toward Nicole who was beaming with a smile.

The
End

About BJ Wane

I live in the Midwest with my husband and our Goldendoodle. I love dogs, enjoy spending time with my daughter, grandchildren, reading and working puzzles.

We have traveled extensively throughout the states, Canada and just once overseas, but I now much prefer being homebody.

I worked for a while writing articles for a local magazine but soon found my interest in writing for myself peaking.

My first book was strictly spanking erotica, but I slowly evolved to writing steamy romance with a touch of suspense. My favorite genre to read is suspense.

I love hearing from readers. Feel free to contact me at bjwane@cox.net with questions or comments.

Contact BJ Wane

My Website

www.bjwaneauthor.com

My E-mail

bjwane@cox.net

Facebook

www.www.facebook.com/bj.wane

www.facebook.com/BJWaneAuthor

Twitter

www.twitter.com/bj_wane

Instagram

www.instagram.com/bjwaneauthor

Goodreads

www.bit.ly/2S6Yg9F

Bookbub

www.bookbub.com/profile/bj-wane

More Books by BJ Wane

VIRGINIA BLUEBLOODS SERIES
Blindsided
Bind Me to You
Surrender to Me
Blackmailed
Bound by Two

MURDER ON MAGNOLIA ISLAND TRILOGY
Logan
Hunter
Ryder

MIAMI MASTERS SERIES
Bound and Saved
Master Me, Please
Mastering Her Fear
Bound to Submit
His to Master and Own
Theirs To Master

COWBOY DOMS SERIES
Submitting to the Rancher
Submitting to the Sheriff
Submitting to the Cowboy
Submitting to the Lawyer
Submitting to Two Doms
Submitting to the Cattleman
Submitting to the Doctor

COWBOY WOLF SERIES
Gavin (Book 1)
Cody (Book 2)
Drake (Book 3)

DOMS OF MOUNTAIN BEND
Protector (Book 1)
Avenger (Book 2)
Defender (Book 3)
Rescuer (Book 4)
Possessor (Book 5)
Redeemer (Book 6)
Vindicator (Book 7)

THE KINCAID SERIES
Resisting Allie (Book 1)
Resisting Lily (Book 2)

SINGLE TITLES
Claiming Mia
Masters of the Castle: Witness Protection Program
Dangerous Interference
Returning to Her Master
Her Master at Last